Praise for ?

"Arguably Cahill's best work to
-Library Of A Viking

"Cahill has gold flowing through his fingertips."
-Wolfmantula

*"A blood-soaked, action-packed journey into the heart of loss
and revenge."*
-FanFiAddict

"It's bloody. It's brutal. It's brilliant."
-Dominish Books

"A story, and series, that just simply deserves to be seen."
-The Wulver's Library

THE EXILE

By Ryan Cahill

THE BOUND AND THE BROKEN

NOVELS

Of Blood and Fire
Of Darkness and Light

NOVELLAS

The Fall
The Exile

THE EXILE

THE BOUND AND THE BROKEN NOVELLA

RYAN CAHILL

THE EXILE

THE BOUND AND THE BROKEN NOVELLA

ISBN 978-1-7396209-0-5

www.ryancahillauthor.com

Edited by: Sarah Chorn
Illustrations by: Aron Cahill
Map by Keir Scott-Schrueder

To Robin, there will never be another like you.

Foreword

When creating *The Bound and The Broken* series I wanted to give readers a world to become completely lost in. A world so rich with history and lore you could feel it dripping off the pages. But this world is my passion, I couldn't simply imply its vast history, that just wouldn't do. I needed to show you.

Set alongside the main books in the series, this is where novellas like *The Exile* come in. *The Exile* is focused around the life of Dayne Ateres before his appearance in *Of Darkness and Light.* Each part of the novella is set at a different point in Dayne's life, each exploring pivotal moments that crafted who he is. Dayne's exploits pre-*Of Darkness and Light* could take up an entire trilogy in and of themselves, but by making this a novella I am able to explore the truly big moments for him, providing you with some extra lore, without eating into the time of the main series.

*Note: this is a companion novella, not a standalone novella. I would very much advise that previous books in the series should be read before starting *The Exile*.*

READING ORDER

The reading order for The Bound and The Broken series is a highly contested thing. So, keeping that in mind, I have decided to provide you with two suggested reading orders. Both are named after sword movements within the series.

If you prefer to jump headfirst into a world, letting the action and high stakes consume you, then the svidarya is the path for you.

If you are the kind of reader who prefers a slower burn, immersing yourself completely in a world, learning the intricacies and terminology as you go, then the fellensír is the correct course.

SVIDARYA

The Fall
Of Blood and Fire
Of Darkness and Light
The Exile

FELLENSÍR

Of Blood and Fire
The Fall
Of Darkness and Light
The Exile

CONTENTS

Sea
of
Stone

ar Nasla

catagan

Dead Rocks
hold

highrass

Kolmir

Khergan

Merchants
Reach

Lightning Coast

Elkenrim

Steeple

Oberona   Greenhills

Gildor

Bromis

O R I A

holm

Ravensgate

M A R D O R U R

Arginwatch

Easterlock

he Burnt Lands

corverstille

L Y N A R I O N

Mountains

The Darkwood   Kingspass

A R A

Argonan
Marshes   falstide

Driftstone

fearsall   Baylomon

Aylia

Veloran Ocean

narrith

Stonehelm

heart
stead   lensa

Cardend

Karvos

Firane

tower
of Aragorn

A R K A L E N   Aerilon

yarrin

Seaside   The Stormwood   Bayfort

Land's End

R I A

PART 1

THE NIGHT OF SMOKE AND ASHES

I

BY BLADE AND BY BLOOD

Skyfell, Valtara
Year 3068 after doom

Dayne leaned forward, resting his arms on the smooth stone ledge. The wind swept a chill across his exposed skin as he looked out at a sky full of wyverns. Wingbeats blended with the whistling rushes of air as the regal creatures swooped past the keep of Redstone and down the cliff face, twisting and turning effortlessly. In the distance, the remnant glow of the setting sun receded past the horizon, shimmering off the wyverns' polished scales and casting the Antigan Ocean in a deep orange hue.

Pulling his eyes from the scene, Dayne looked at his little sister, Alina, who sat on the ledge, her feet dangling, her eyes wide and jaw slackened. She absently played with the sapphire pendant that hung from her neck.

"That'll be me one day," Alina said, not taking her eyes from the wyverns. "I'll be a wyvern rider. Just like mother. You will too, Mera."

Dayne shifted his gaze to Mera, who stood on Alina's other side, a broad smile on her face, her hand clasped to the back of Alina's robes. The sides of Mera's head were shaved, her long brown hair tied into a plait, her blue eyes glistening in the incandescent light of the sinking sun. She was beautiful, though she never liked when he called her that. But that didn't stop him from thinking it.

After a few moments, Mera looked up, catching Dayne's eye, her smile turning to laughter.

"What?" Alina turned her head back and forth between Mera and Dayne, a touch of annoyance creeping into her voice. "Why are you laughing? What's so funny?"

Dayne forced down a laugh at the scowl etched into his little sister's face. She may have only seen twelve summers, but she had the ferocity of a seasoned warrior. He reached out and ruffled the hair at the back of Alina's head, much to her irritation. "Nothing, Alina," he said, shaking his head. "There is not a doubt in my mind that you will be the greatest wyvern rider who ever lived."

Alina narrowed her eyes and pursed her lips, her scowl intensifying as though she were trying to determine if Dayne was lying. Then, as though satisfied with his answer, she let out a slight *hmmph*, turning her gaze back to the wyverns, her eyes flitting to and fro as she traced the creatures' movements in the sky.

Catching Mera's eye, Dayne shook his head and rolled his eyes. The soft smile he received in return set a warmth in his bones.

They stood in Dayne's father's study for what felt like hours, gazing out the wide window, watching as the orange glow faded as it was replaced by the silvery wash of the full moon, its cold light glittering off the ocean below. And Dayne would have stood there even longer had he not heard the sound of the door opening behind them.

"Alina Ateres. Is it not long past your bedtime, young lady?" Dayne recognised his father's voice even before he turned to see the tall, wiry man stepping through the doorway behind them, arms crossed.

As though ignoring their father, Alina continued to stare at the ocean. She tilted her chin slightly higher in defiance, folding her arms across her chest. The sight of it nearly caused Dayne to break out in another fit of laughter.

"*Alina*?"

"Dayne said—" Alina didn't get the chance to finish her sentence as Arkin Ateres tucked his hands beneath her armpits and hoisted her up, tossing her slightly and spinning her so she faced him.

"What did Dayne say?" Arkin raised an eyebrow, his eyes fixed on Alina as she dangled in front of him, daring her to lie.

"He said I could stay up to watch the sunset," Alina answered, trying in vain to re-fold her arms across her chest. Dayne recognised the familiar stubborn glint in her eyes. "And the wyverns."

"Oh, did he now?" Arkin pulled Alina into his chest, allowing his daughter's arms to loop around his neck and her legs to wrap around his torso.

Dayne shrugged, shaking his head. "She just kept asking… and asking… *and asking*. It was less trouble to just say yes."

Arkin laughed, raising an eyebrow as he looked at Alina, who now clung to him like a monkey, her expression the image of innocence. "Is that so? Only twelve summers and you already have your brothers wrapped around your fingers. You take after your mother." Shifting Alina to his left, Arkin turned to look at Mera. "And your part in all of this, Mera?"

"I was only ensuring that neither of them got into any trouble, my lord." Mera bowed slightly at the waist.

"Enough of that," Arkin said, frowning, waving his hand at Mera. "Go bow at some old man who begs it of you."

Without a moment's hesitation, Mera dipped her shoulders once more, the slightest beginnings of a grin touching the corners of her mouth. "*Of course*, my lord. As you wish."

Arkin furrowed his brow and lowered Alina to the ground. "If you're quite done. Could you please take Alina to her chambers? The sunset has been and gone. I will ensure she awakes in time to see it rise. Right now, I could use a word with my son."

Alina made to argue, but one look from Arkin let her know it was better not to.

"Of course, my lord." Mera nodded her head, then moved towards Dayne, pulling him into a brief embrace and whispering in his ear. "I'll still be awake when you're finished."

Dayne's pulse quickened, his mouth instantly turning as dry as sand.

When Mera pulled away, she kept her eyes locked on Dayne's before taking Alina's hand and leading her past the heavy wooden desk and the three soft couches in the middle of the study, closing the doors behind them.

"I like her," Arkin said, walking past Dayne and leaning on the window ledge. "She's got spirit. And she's got heart."

Silence filled the air as Dayne rested his elbows on the ledge beside his father, staring out at the ocean. Only the crashing waves and the occasional gusts of wind as wyverns swept across the rock face dared interrupt the absence of sound.

"It will begin in three days' time." Arkin didn't turn to look at Dayne. Instead, he simply stared out at the horizon, exhaling deeply through his nostrils.

"So soon?" Dayne could do nothing to hide his surprise. He knew the rebellion was close, but he had thought weeks, not days. His fingers tapped involuntarily against the stone ledge. "We're not ready. We need more time."

"We will always want for time, Dayne. That is the human way. We would die waiting for the perfect moment that will never come. There is only now. We have spoken to the others, and they have agreed. Houses Thebal, Deringal, and Herak will support us. Vakira and Koraklon will wait and likely choose the winning side. Your mother is arranging the last pieces. She is at Stormwatch now, meeting with the fleet captains. We will not make the same mistakes as those before us. We will take back Valtara, fortify the Hot Gates, and rip the Lorian ships from the ocean. We will be free, my son. I promise."

Dayne didn't speak. He simply nodded, turning his gaze towards the crashing waves hundreds of feet below. Once they started this, there would be no going back. The Lorian Empire had let Valtara live after the first rebellion, but if they failed a second time… Alina's face flashed through Dayne's mind. Her laugh, her smile, her joy. She had only seen twelve summers, and Baren only eighteen. He would not let them to grow up with a Lorian boot on their necks. Dayne had only seen two more summers than Baren, but Baren was still his little brother. Dayne's jaw clenched as he thought of the brother he had never met – Owain. The brother the empire had taken as tribute, just as they did to every first-born male in Valtara since the last rebellion. He would not let that happen to his children, nor Alina's, nor Baren's. He would rather die fighting for his freedom than live in chains. "I'm ready."

"I know you are, my son." Arkin rested a hand on Dayne's shoulder. "And it will be an honour to fight by your side."

"By blade and by blood."

"By blade and by blood," Arkin repeated. "You should get some sleep. You will not get many good nights once this begins."

Dayne nodded absently, resting his hand atop his father's. "I will, shortly."

Arkin took Dayne's face into his hands and planted a kiss on Dayne's forehead before pulling him into an embrace so tight he felt his bones creak. "I love you, Dayne… All four of you." Arkin pulled away before resting his forehead against Dayne's and locking their gazes.

"We know, Father. And we love you too. I am proud to be of House Ateres, proud to bear the sigil of the wyvern."

A weak smile touched Arkin's lips, and he pulled Dayne into an embrace once more, then made for the door without another word.

Dayne watched his father leave before turning back towards the window, resting his hands on the ledge until his heart settled to a slow, methodical thump. With one last look over the silver-painted ocean waves, Dayne turned and left.

The corridors of Redstone were empty save for the occasional patrol of the Redstone guard and the odd servant finishing up the last of their daily tasks. The flickering flames of oil lamps illuminated the red stone walls and floors, casting criss-cross shadows where the light was broken by long stretches of fluted columns.

There was little Dayne could do to keep the smile from his face as he made his way to Mera's chambers. He was almost there when he was hit by a sudden realisation. Letting out a sigh, he stopped. "I should check on Alina…" The nights he didn't check on Alina and plant a kiss on her forehead always led to him having to face the wrath of her tiny fists the next morning. She was small, but fierce. "Gods damn it."

Dayne turned on his heels, picking up his pace. He took a right, then a left at the end of the corridor, left again, then descended the flight of stairs beside the library door, following the walkway across to the other side of the keep. He was almost at Alina's chambers when he heard the knocking.

Knock. Knock.

"My lady Alina. Your father calls for you."

Dayne froze. That voice was not Valtaran. It was close, as though it had been practised meticulously, but there was something off about it. What's more, if Dayne's father had wanted Alina, he would have come to her himself. Dayne pressed himself against the wall, peeking around the corner.

Two guards stood outside the thick wooden doors of Alina's chambers, a man and a woman. Each wore the bronzed cuirass and burnt orange skirts of the Redstone guard, along with a pair of greaves and a bronze helmet in the typical Valtaran style – covering most of their face, with almond-shaped slits for eyes and a thin opening that dropped sharply from their nose to the base of the helmet. They each held the circular ordo shield in their left hand with a long ash wood valyna gripped tightly in their right.

Through the helmets, Dayne couldn't get a look at their faces, but he knew one thing: they were not Redstone guard. Their accents would have been enough, but their forearms were bare. They held no markings of the spear or the sword. Dayne glanced down at his own forearms. Two circles of black ink wrapped around both his left and his right. Right for the spear, left for the blade. No man nor women was permitted into the Redstone guard without at least two markings in either the spear or the blade.

Dayne patted his hip, realising he had no weapons with him, not even so much as a knife.

"Lady Alina?" The woman rapped her knuckles on the wood, harder. Her voice growing colder, firmer.

A few moments of silence were followed by a creaking sound as one of the doors began to open. "Father? But it's so late?"

Dayne's chest emptied. "Alina, no! Close the door!"

He charged, his heart galloping like a horse, his chest trembling. Whatever these imposters wanted with Alina, they would have to climb over his bloody corpse before he would let them touch a hair on her head. No sounds reached his ears save for that of his blood rushing through his veins and his feet slapping against the stone.

His shout had alerted the two imposters to his presence, but they hadn't turned fast enough to stop him. Dayne focused on the man who stood to the right, a look of surprise painted on his face.

Dropping his shoulder, Dayne crashed into the man, connecting with the bronze cuirass with such force it sent a shudder through his body. This was what he imagined it would feel like to collide with a tree trunk. But unlike a tree, this man did not have roots. The sheer strength of Dayne's charge lifted the stranger off his feet, and they both crashed into the wooden doors and through, into Alina's chambers.

The imposter hit the ground first, sending a tremor through Dayne's arms. But the man recovered faster, catching Dayne across the jaw with a quick fist. Panic. That was the only thing that flooded through his veins. Stars and sunspots flitted across his eyes, and his sense of balance shifted. The man tried to throw another fist, but Dayne swung his elbow and caught the imposter in the jaw. *Crack.* His head bounced back against the stone.

His body trembling, Dayne punched down with all his strength, slamming his closed fist into the man's windpipe. Then again, and again. Another *crack* and the imposter clasped his hands to his throat, a gurgling noise escaping, blood spluttering over his lips.

Frantically, Dayne searched for a weapon, scanning the man's body. His fingers fell on the pommel of a sword, still sitting in a sheath strapped to the man's waist. But as Dayne went to yank the sword free, a noise to his left reminded him of the other imposter. He threw himself to the ground, howling as a spear tip sliced through the skin at the side of his neck. Had he moved even a fraction of a second slower, that tip would have plunged straight through, and he would be dining in Achyron's halls.

Dayne rolled as he hit the ground, scrambling to his feet, his lungs burning, blood trickling from the cut on his neck. "Alina, get behind me!"

Alina shrieked as Dayne reached out, pulling her in and shoving her behind him.

"Get back," he roared at Alina, pushing her backwards blindly, not daring to pull his eyes from the woman who stood before them. She was just shy of six feet, with a lean muscular build. The light of the oil lanterns glimmered off her bronzed cuirass, her ordo shield hefted in her left hand, her spear gripped in her fist. She moved like a predator, her eyes narrowed, her knees bent, each step slow and purposeful. She may not have been a Valtaran, but this woman knew death.

"This doesn't have to be difficult," the woman said as she circled to the left, her muscles tensed, her gaze fixed on Dayne's, poised to strike. "I'm not here to kill either of you. I'm here to keep you safe. You need not be part of the bloodshed that is to come."

Dayne said nothing. He didn't dare blink. His heart thumped in his ears. He reached back with his right hand, feeling his fingertips brush the top of Alina's head.

"I won't let her touch you," he whispered, trying his best to reassure his little sister. He would die before he let that woman lay a hand on Alina.

"Dayne, who is she?" A tremble held Alina's voice, sneaking into her words. "I'm scared."

The woman took a step forward.

Dayne took a step back, using his fingertips to push Alina back with him. He met the woman's stare. "I won't let you."

"So be it," the woman replied, her voice deepening into an irritated growl. "I don't have time for this. They only need one of you. Die well."

As the woman stepped forward, raising her spear, Dayne's eyes fell to the man on the ground. He was dead, his arms now sprawled, blood coating his mouth and face. His spear and shield lay beside him, his sword still in its sheath.

The woman lunged, extending her spear, the blade slicing through the air. Dayne reached back and pushed Alina to the ground before dipping out of the way, gasping as the spear sliced across his right shoulder, grazing the bone. He dove towards the ground, rolling as he hit the stone. Rising back to his feet, he slipped his arm through the leather fastening of the dead man's shield, wrapping his fingers around the handle at the edge. More by instinct than anything else, he swung the shield across himself, a dull vibration running through the overlapping bronze and wood as the woman's spear bounced away harmlessly.

Reaching down, Dayne grasped the shaft of the dead man's spear with his free hand, feeling the familiar touch of the smooth ash wood against his palm. Howling, he thrust at the woman's legs just above her grieves. She cried out as steel bit flesh, the spear tip cutting through the side of her leg, just below the knee.

Holding back his fear, Dayne pushed forward, lifting himself upright and ramming his shield into the woman's, attempting to catch her off balance. But she had regained her composure far quicker than he had hoped.

They exchanged blows back and forth, testing each other. Dayne had trained every day from the time he had seen his eighth summer. He knew these weapons like he knew himself. But he had never killed someone with them. He had not lived through a war.

Dayne had sparred thousands of times. He could move through the forms in his sleep, but this was different. One of them would die here.

A scream ripped through the chamber. Dayne dared not take his eyes from his opponent, but the light of the lanterns illuminated a flash and a glint of steel. "Alina, no!"

Alina continued to scream as she rammed the knife into the woman's back. She attempted to yank it free, but the woman swept her shield around, leaving Alina in a heap on the ground, groaning as she attempted to pull herself back to her feet.

Fire roared through Dayne's body as he charged, forgoing all sense of self-preservation. He bashed his shield against the woman's, sending her stumbling backward, but as he raised his spear arm, she pivoted and cracked the butt of her spear into the side of his head, sending him stumbling. His balance deserting him, his fingers released their grip on the spear which clattered to the floor. The woman planted her foot on his shield and kicked down hard. Dazed from the blow to his head, he had loosened his grip on the shield and only the leather arm strap was holding it in place. The rim cracked off his nose, and his vision exploded in blinding light. He collapsed to the ground, blood filling his nostrils, the woman's spear tip pressed against his neck.

"This is your last chance," she said, her hand unwavering as the steel of the spear pressed against Dayne's neck. "Don't make me take any more lives than I have to."

Instinctively, Dayne reached out to the Spark, feeling the elemental strands pulsate through the fabric of the world, radiating power. He let the energy surge through him, his mother's words echoing in his mind. *Nobody can know what you can do. Nobody, Dayne. If the empire finds out you can touch the Spark, they will drag you from these walls kicking and screaming. They will either kill you or train you to kill your own.*

Even as the words filled his head, Dayne pulled on threads of Air. He had no choice.

The sound of footsteps filled Dayne's ears, and the woman spun, sweeping her spear through the air, the shaft colliding with another as a soldier charged through the doors of the room. The newcomer swept the woman aside, driving his spear through her gut. Before she could do so much as scream, he pulled his sword free from its sheath, cleaving her spear arm at the elbow and driving the blade through her exposed throat. The woman collapsed in a clatter of metal on stone, gasping for air, her blood seeping out onto the floor like spilt wine.

His entire body trembling, Dayne pulled his eyes from the floundering woman and looked towards the soldier who had saved him. Four rings on each arm, bisected by a black line. A blademaster and a spearmaster both. Even in Valtara that was rare.

The man dropped to one knee and pulled his closed fist across his chest. "My lord Ateres, your father sent me to find you. We must go now."

Relief seeped into Dayne's bones as he recognised his saviour: Marlin Arkon, Steward of House Ateres.

"You took your time." Dayne released his grip on the handle of his shield and pulled his hand free, the shield clattering to the ground. He brought his hand to the side of his head, feeling the blood tack against his skin. "My father, where is he? What is happening?"

"He went to rouse the men. Someone has betrayed us. The empire has assaulted the keep, I—"

Marlin was cut short by the sound of Alina's voice as she crashed into Dayne, wrapping her arms around him, sobbing. "Dayne, what's happening? Are you all right? Where's Mother and Father?"

"I'm all right, little monkey." Dayne gritted his teeth as he spoke, his wounds burning, his head throbbing. "Everything will be all right." Dayne closed his eyes and leaned his head into Alina's, trying as best he could to reassure her. Peeling open his eyes, he picked up his shield once more and turned his attention back to Marlin. "Where is Baren?"

"I sent some of the guards to protect your brother. They should have reached him about the same time I reached you."

"We need to get to him. I need to know he is all right."

Dayne's heart slowed to a steady beat as they ran down the corridor towards Baren's chambers.

"Dayne! Alina!"

Relief flooded through Dayne at the sound of his brother's voice. Ahead, Baren and three Redstone guards were sprinting down the corridor towards Dayne, Alina, and Marlin. Baren scooped Alina up in one arm as he reached them, before pulling Dayne in close. "You're both all right. Thank the gods." Baren held the embrace for a few moments before letting Alina down and turning back to Dayne. "What is happening? Two guards came to my quarters. They said Father wanted to see me. They wore the armour of the Redstone guard, but they were no Valtarans."

"Somebody has betrayed us," Dayne replied. "The empire knows about the rebellion."

"Who would do that? Why would—"

"It doesn't matter who or why, not now. You need to take Alina and go with Marlin to father's office. Take the passage down to the cliffs and get out of the city. There is a small cave at the very base of the cliff's edge. Go there and wait."

Baren's eyes widened. "I'm not running, Dayne! I can help."

"I know you can," Dayne said, resting his hand on his brother's shoulder. "But there is more than one way to help. I don't want you to run – I want you to get Alina somewhere safe, to protect our sister. What if something were to happen to her?"

"I can help too!" came a defiant squeak.

Dayne smiled as he looked down to find Alina glaring back at him, her eyes narrowed. She had as much heart as any soldier he knew. She would make a fine warrior one day. "Not today, little monkey."

An irritated grunt was her only reply.

"I need you to protect her," Dayne said, turning his attention back to Baren.

For a moment, Dayne thought his brother might argue. But then, without letting his stare waver, Baren nodded. "What will you do?"

"I will find Father and Mother. We will drive the empire back, then I will come and find you."

Baren nodded once more, then knelt beside Alina, whispering in her ear as she sobbed.

Dragging his eyes from his siblings, Dayne turned to Marlin. "Marlin."

"Yes, my lord."

"Keep them safe."

"On my life."

"No." Dayne reached out, grasping Marlin's forearm. "I would very much prefer if you kept yourself safe as well."

The faintest hint of a smile touched the corner of Marlin's mouth. "I'll do what I can, my lord. At least take the guard with you," he said, gesturing to the three Redstone guards who had come with Baren.

Dayne nodded, indicating for the guards to come with him. He almost stumbled as Marlin pulled on his arm and dragged him into an embrace. "War is no different to peace. It is simply more honest. Do not hesitate, do not contemplate mercy. Remember everything I have taught you."

Dayne pulled Marlin in tighter until it felt as though his arms would give way. Along with Dayne's father, Marlin had been his mentor ever since he could first hold a sword. "I will remember, by blade and by blood."

"Go," Marlin said, pulling away. "I will keep them safe."

The shouts and cries of battle rose into the night as Dayne and the Redstone guards reached the balcony that over-looked the gardens of the keep. Below, a brownish-red flagstone pathway bisected the gardens, framed by rows of enormous orange trees; the vibrant colour of their fruit was striking against the green of the leaves. Near the centre of the garden, just over a hundred Valtaran warriors stood side by side, their ordo shields interlocked, bracing against the tide of imperial soldiers that flooded in through the open gates.

At any other time, the sight of imperial soldiers charging into the Redstone gardens would have set fear in Dayne's heart. But then, as he looked out over the fighting, fire burned in his veins. The empire must have hoped to take the keep while the garrison slept, taking Dayne and his siblings to use against their parents. But now, they stood against a wall of Valtaran shields. Not only that, but they stood against the finest warriors House Ateres had to offer: the Andurii.

Masters of both the blade and the spear, the Andurii were the beating heart of the Ateres army, and they were led by none other than Arkin Ateres himself.

Each of the Andurii were garbed in bronzed cuirasses of hardened steel, matching greaves and vambraces, crests of bone-white horse hair running from the front of their helmets to the back, cloaks of burnt-orange draped over their shoulders. Blades were strapped to each of their hips, thick-shafted valynas gripped in their fists, and the wyvern of House Ateres emblazoned across their shields.

The hairs along Dayne's arms stood on end, and fire burned brightly in his veins as he watched the imperial soldiers crashing against the Andurii shields, a trickling stream meeting a mountain. Except this mountain moved; slowly and precisely, it forced the intruders back towards the gates. Bodies fell with each step. Andurii spears from the second row found flesh and bone, while the first row held their shields with unwavering discipline, relentlessly pushing the imperial soldiers back. With a knot in his throat, Dayne looked to the far right of the Andurii formation, for that was where his father would be. The far right of a shield wall's front line was the most vulnerable link in the chain, and so that was where the most seasoned warrior took position. His father's voice echoed in his mind. *A true leader, Dayne, leads by example, not by command.*

A tingle ran from the nape of Dayne's neck all the way down his spine, every hair on his body standing on end. The sensation gave barely a second's warning before threads of Earth and Air streamed from somewhere within the imperial ranks. *An Imperial Battlemage.*

As soon as Dayne spotted the woman, blonde hair tied back with string, black cloak billowing behind her, the threads seeped into the ground beneath the Andurii lines. "No, Father—"

Men and women were thrown into the air as the ground beneath the Andurii erupted in a plume of earth and stone. The force of the blast was so violent, it tore trees from the ground, the walls trembled, and the air itself seemed to ripple.

Dayne doubled over, coughing and spluttering as his lungs dragged in the dirt that had been lifted into the air. Cries of agony rang out through the dust-occluded night, the empty groans of men and women who would soon be drawing their last breaths.

Releasing his shield, Dayne rubbed at his eyes, trying to rid them of the tacky mixture of dirt and sweat. But as his vision returned, his heart sank. The blast had ripped a hole through the Andurii lines and taken many of the imperial soldiers with them as well. Bodies lay broken: bones shattered, limbs twisted, armour crushed.

Only a handful of the Andurii had survived. They dragged themselves to their feet and formed a new shield wall, fifteen wide in the front line, twelve in the second. More imperial soldiers flooded through the gates, swarming around the woman wearing the flowing black cloak, washing over the bodies of the dead.

"My lord, are you hurt?" One of the Redstone guards rested a hand on Dayne's back. The man's face was coated in dirt, streaks of blood and sweat carving paths through the grime.

"Sound the bells!" Dayne shouted, pushing the guard away. "We need archers on the walls *now*. Tear those imperials to ribbons."

"Yes, my lord." The man's eyes gleamed in the moonlight, loss and anger rising within them. His jaw clenched, he nodded, then turned and sprinted back towards the keep.

Dayne turned to the remaining two guards beside him. "We need to shut those gates."

Gripping the shaft of his spear tighter, he made his way from the balcony to the connecting corridor and out onto the walls that ran along the western flank of the garden.

Just over thirty soldiers stood on the western wall between him and the gatehouse, the clang of steel-on-steel ringing through the night. It was absolute chaos. Each warrior wore the bronze cuirasses and burnt orange skirts of the Redstone guard, but they hacked and slashed at each other like rabid wolves. "Look at their markings!" Dayne bellowed to the two guards who charged with him. "The imposters do not bear Valtaran markings."

Dayne didn't get the chance to see if the guards had heard him. Two of the soldiers closest to him charged. Their arms were unmarked. Dayne held his breath for a moment, settling his fear. In a daze from the blast, he had left his shield where he had dropped it. The temptation to reach for the Spark was immense, but he subdued it.

Pulling his arm back, Dayne howled, launching his spear through the air, a blazing fire igniting within him. The spear caught one of the soldiers in the chest, the weight of the blow throwing him off balance, his screams echoing through the night as he fell from the wall.

The other soldier continued her charge, shield raised across her torso awkwardly, spear held underhand at her side. This soldier was not like the one who had come for Alina. She had been lethal. This soldier, however, wasn't used to holding Valtaran weapons. The ordo was nothing like the rectangular shields the imperial soldiers were accustomed to. It was made specifically for use in a Valtaran shield wall, though through years of training, could be wielded just as effectively in single combat. This woman had not had years of training.

She struck upward with the spear. Dayne dropped his left shoulder, wrapped both his hands around the shaft of the spear, and rammed his right shoulder into the woman's shield. As she stumbled backwards, Dayne yanked the spear free from her grip, pivoted, and pushed forward.

The woman staggered backwards, tripping over a body that lay limp on the rampart. Dayne leapt forward as she fell. He lifted his foot and slammed it down where her arm met her shoulder, hearing a violent *snap* as he pinned her arm against the rim of her shield, the bone cracking under the weight, breaking through skin, blood sluicing. The wail that left her mouth chilled Dayne's blood.

Dayne lifted his spear to her throat.

"No, no, please!"

Hesitation leads to lives lost. Marlin's words echoed in Dayne's mind.

"May The Mother embrace you." In one smooth motion, Dayne slid the tip of his spear into the woman's throat. The motion was swift, but the look in her eyes would be carved into his mind until time broke. *Better to die quick.*

Inch by inch, Dayne and the two Redstone guard fought their way along the western wall. Four more joined their side, but for every imperial soldier they killed, two emerged from the gatehouse, these ones garbed in the red and black leathers of the Lorian Empire.

Dayne glanced down at the gardens. Only fifteen Andurii still stood. They were clustered together, a slight bend in their line to help protect their flanks. Bodies littered the ground around them, twisted up in the branches of fallen trees, blood flowing freely. The Imperial Battlemage stood about twenty feet back, watching; she had played her part.

Pivoting, Dayne avoided a spear aimed at his gut, then drove the tip of his own valyna through his attacker's throat, letting the man stagger backwards off the ramparts.

The sonorous chime of bells resounded through the gardens, echoing off stone, ringing in Dayne's ears. Calls and shouts followed, more Redstone guard pouring from the keep, filling the balconies, charging onto the ramparts, nocking and loosing arrows as they moved. Within moments, steel rained down into the gardens, slicing through leather and sundering flesh. *That will buy the Andurii more time.* Only twelve Andurii still stood, clutches of Redstone guard standing at their flanks. Even with the archers' support, the Lorian tide would soon wash over them. He needed to close those gates.

Reluctantly, Dayne pulled his gaze back to what was in front of him. Imperial soldiers now clogged the walls, more charging onto the ramparts with each passing moment. Some wore the armour of the Redstone guard, but most were garbed in the red and black leathers of the Lorian Empire, sharp steel in their fists.

Six guards now stood by Dayne's side, wounded and bloody, but not broken. If he called for a shield wall, they would likely be able to push the soldiers back, crushing them against the weight of their own charge, forcing them off the edges of the ramparts. But if he did that, they would never reach the gatehouse in time; his father and the Andurii would be overrun, cut down like blades of grass. Nor could he simply carve his way through. Every Valtaran warrior was worth ten of the imperial soldiers, but there were simply too many. Fate, it seemed, had stripped his choice from him. "Forgive me, Mother."

Opening his mind, Dayne reached out to the Spark, feeling its power surge through him. He would not let his father die. Not when he had the power to save him. Dayne pulled on threads of Air, dragging them into himself, feeling their cool touch prickle at his skin. He pulled harder, welling the threads together, forming a ball. He needed to clear the Lorian soldiers from the wall.

A piercing shriek ripped through the night, its harsh echo lingering. The first shriek was answered by one or two more, then by fifteen or twenty, then hundreds, until the sound was the only thing Dayne could hear. Dayne's heart stopped, and he released his hold on the Spark. A defiant fire burned in his blood. He knew that sound.

Wyverns.

Flashes of colour whipped past the walls and burst free from the dark clouds above, gusts of wind following in their wake.

Screams and shouts rose from the gardens and the walls as dozens of winged creatures descended on the imperial forces, tearing through flesh, rending steel, and cleaving bone. The riders who sat astride the great beasts launched spears into the thick of bodies, splitting leather and spraying blood. Each of the wyverns was at least the size of a large war horse, armoured in scales of varying colours, thick forelimbs stretching into leathery wings, obsidian talons glistening in the moonlight.

Dayne watched as a large wyvern, scales of deep blue, crashed down in front of the Battlemage. The creature spread its wings wide, its lips pulling back in a snarl, its hulking frame looming over the woman. Dayne felt the mage reach for the Spark, threads of Fire and Air wheeling around her. But before she could unleash her devastation, the wyvern arched its neck and clamped its jaws around her torso, its razor-sharp teeth tearing through her armour as if it were made of clay. The woman let out a blood-chilling wail as the wyvern thrashed its head side to side, shredding her armour, ripping her flesh, spraying the air with her life's blood. Her screams rose above everything else, high-pitched and shrill, forcing all other sounds to yield. Dayne could feel the visceral pain in her cries, a shiver running through his body. He looked away, his stomach turning. And then it stopped. When Dayne looked back, the large wyvern had moved on, lifting itself into the air before dropping back down into a clutch of Lorian soldiers, claws swiping, tail snapping left and right.

The night took on an eerie stillness as Dayne looked out over the walls and the gardens, the sound of clashing steel and war cries replaced by crunching bone, weeping, and the soft melancholy groans of the dying. The imperial soldiers were in full retreat through the gates, leaving the dead and injured behind to meet The Mother. Even the walls were nearly empty. Crumpled heaps of flesh and twisted bone coated the battlements, barely recognisable from the men and women they had once been. Dayne had never seen the aftermath of a wyvern attack. The creatures were as merciless and savage as they were beautiful.

Swallowing the knot in his throat, Dayne stepped through the mess of mutilated bodies, forcing himself to look down at the faces of the dead, their eyes cold, devoid of life. He hoped he would never die that way.

Behind him, he could hear the thrusts of cold steel as the Redstone guard drove their spear tips into any poor unfortunate souls who had survived the wyverns. Sparing them the pain may have been the merciful thing to do, but Dayne couldn't stomach it again. He kept walking, making his way towards the staircase that led down to the gardens.

As Dayne stepped off the staircase that led from the ramparts, a massive wyvern descended into the gardens, spirals of dust lifting into the air with every wingbeat. The creature's scales were dark red, almost black, flecked with spots of gold at the edges. Its muscles rippled as it lowered itself and spread its wings, allowing its rider to step down onto solid ground. Dayne's feet carrying him forward, he kept his gaze locked on the rider and wyvern as they touched foreheads. Then, the rider removed her helmet and turned towards Dayne. What started as a tentative step quickly turned to a full sprint until Dayne and the woman collided, wrapping their arms around each other.

"My boy." Dayne's mother cupped his cheeks in her hands, pulling back, staring into his eyes, the most relieved of smiles spreading across her face. Once more she pulled him in close, whispering, "You're all right." She let out a sigh, as though a weight had lifted from her shoulders, her voice softening. "You're all right…"

After what seemed like hours, Ilya Ateres stepped back, her hands clasping Dayne's shoulders. "Baren and Alina?"

"They're all right. Marlin took them through the passage at the back of father's study. He's keeping them safe."

Dayne's mother nodded, her tongue running across her lips as though she were contemplating something.

"Nice of you to arrive."

Both Dayne and his mother turned at the sound of Arkin Ateres's voice. Dayne's father wore the bronzed steel armour of the Andurii, the Wyvern of House Ateres emblazoned in white across his breastplate. Blood and dirt stained his skin and tacked his hair to his forehead, he limped heavily, favouring his right leg, and his arm was draped around the shoulder of another man who wore the armour of the Andurii – Savrin Vander, the Champion of House Ateres.

"Come here," Arkin said, lifting his arm from Savrin's shoulders and pulling Dayne and his mother into a tight embrace. He kissed Dayne's forehead before clasping his hand around the back of Ilya's neck. Dayne could hear him whisper, "I thought I had lost you."

"And I you," Ilya whispered back, the corner of her mouth rising in a weak smile that met a creeping tear.

"Your brother and sister?" An ocean of desperation filled his father's eyes.

"They're safe. They're with Marlin."

"You did well, my son." Dayne's father pulled away, grunting, his breath raspy. He swept his gaze over the blood-stained, corpse-filled gardens.

"They came for us in our chambers – Alina, Baren, and me. Were it not for Marlin, they would have succeeded."

"They came for you? Why would they come for our children?" Anger permeated Dayne's mother's voice, her hand falling to the sword at her hip.

Dayne's father turned back, resting his hand on Ilya's shoulder. "They seek to crush the rebellion while maintaining a hold on Valtara's future. If they control the heirs to the Houses, they control everything. There isn't much time. The empire learned of our plans and have moved more swiftly than we could have ever imagined. We need to push this advantage while we still have it. We need the full might of the House armoured and ready. We—"

A roar unlike anything Dayne had ever heard shook the air, rumbling like thunder. Every head in the garden turned towards the sky. What burst from the charcoal clouds set an implacable fear in Dayne's heart. A dragon so large it blotted out the light of the moon.

The creature plummeted to the ground at an impossible speed, keeping its enormous wings tucked at its side until the last moment. The dragon crashed down on top of Dayne's mother's wyvern, Thandril, its claws wrapping around Thandril's head and slamming him into the ground. The stone shook and oranges fell from the trees, splitting as they cracked against the blood-stained ground below. Thandril thrashed, struggling to break free from the enormous dragon's hold, screeching as the dragon's talons tore through his scales.

Dayne's mother screamed, a shriek that chilled the blood in his veins, as visceral as the mage's had been when she was torn apart.

"Ilya, no!" Dayne's father reached out but was too late to stop Dayne's mother from surging towards the dragon, her sword drawn. A mortal charging towards a god.

The creature lifted its head, muscle rippling beneath its powerful neck, the light of the moon revealing the dark brown colouring of its scales. It was only then that Dayne could truly see the sheer size of the monster. Its wings spread across the breadth of the garden. Its body stood over a hundred feet from head to tail. Ridges of horns framed its face and neck. Its teeth shone in the light of the moon, like swords of alabaster dripping crimson. A warrior sat on the creature's back, where the neck met the body, garbed in gleaming white plate, a black flame emblazoned across their breast. *The Dragonguard.*

For a long moment, Dayne watched as his mother streaked across the courtyard, charging towards the beast. He watched as the dragon turned its head, and he watched as it craned its neck down and unleashed a column of fire.

Flames poured from the dragon's jaws like a raging river, consuming everything in their path, incinerating the air, turning skin to ash, melting steel. Screams rose and were snuffed out in an instant. Then, abruptly, before the flames reached Ilya, they flickered from existence as the dragon unleashed a monstrous roar, rearing onto its hind legs. In the light of the dying fire, Dayne could see Thandril raking his talons along the dragon's underbelly, slicing through its scales, blood spilling from long wounds.

Regaining its composure, the dragon slammed its claw back down onto Thandril's head, sending furrows snaking through the stone. The enormous beast clamped its jaws around Thandril's neck, its teeth cracking through the wyvern's scales.

In one powerful motion, the monstrous creature ripped Thandril's head free from his body, tossing it to the ground before unleashing a roar so visceral it shook the air. The brief flash of hope that had begun to kindle in Dayne's heart was snuffed out in an instant.

Mid-stride, Dayne's mother stopped, as though Thandril's death had severed a chord within her. She dropped to her knees, releasing her hold on her sword, letting the steel clatter against the stone.

"Ilya!" Dayne's father rushed past him, barely allowing his right leg to touch the ground with each stride, then dropped to Ilya's side.

"Lay down your weapons," a woman's voice boomed, echoing throughout the gardens, bouncing off the stone and clinging to the air. Dayne didn't have to look to know that it came from the warrior who sat astride the dragon. Threads of Air and Spirit whirled around her, amplifying her voice. "Lay them down now and I will not extinguish your bloodlines and burn this city to ash."

A series of roars rolled through the skies above like thunder. Dayne tilted his head to see streams of fire illuminating the charcoal clouds like cracks of orange lightning and the dark shapes of wyverns dropping from the sky. *More dragons.*

The dragon before them bent its forelimbs and leaned across Thandril's crumpled body, lowering its neck. Steadying herself with threads of Air, the warrior slid from the dragon's back, landing softly on her feet. "You have lost," the woman said, her voice all measure of calm. She continued forward until she was only a few feet from Dayne's mother and father, the blend of pale moonlight and the orange-red flicker of the dying flames around them shimmering off her white plate. "Arkin and Ilya Ateres. You are charged with plotting to destroy the peace and inciting rebellion." As the woman spoke, her dragon lifted its head into the air and spread its wings wide, blood dripping from its jaws, its eyes blazing orange.

"You will pay for what you have done," the woman continued. "But your children need not. Lay down your weapons now, and we will spare their lives. Do not, and I will drag the air from their lungs myself."

His arms still wrapped around Ilya, Arkin turned his head, his eyes red and welling with tears. He held Dayne's gaze, swallowed, then let his shoulders sag, his sword dropping to the ground with a clatter.

II

THE EXILE

Dayne shifted his knees, steadying himself as the ship rocked from side to side, moving with the ebb and flow of the waves. His parents knelt on either side of him, hands bound, heads bowed. His mother stared vacantly at the ground, expressionless.

Ahead, a sheer rock face rose from the ocean, sprawling right and left, blending into the night. Nestled in the rock-face, thousands of feet above the ocean, with walls twice the size of Skyfell's and towers that loomed over the dark waters, was the fortress city of Stormwatch – the focal point of Valtaran naval control across the Antigan ocean.

Hundreds of orange lights illuminated the city, burning in the night: candles sitting in windows, lanterns hanging along the battlements, the flame of the lighthouse burning at the very top of the keep. Even though he could not make them out at that distance, Dayne had no doubts that the city's battlements were teeming with soldiers who, at that moment, were staring out at the fleet of lion-bannered Lorian ships that approached.

Dayne tugged at the ropes that bound his hands behind his back and cut into his wrists. He could have reached out to the Spark and removed them in a matter of seconds, but the Dragonguard who had captured them stood at the bow, her helmet in the crook of her arm, her dark hair whipping out behind her. She would sense him the very second he touched the Spark. And then she would most likely kill him, or worse, take him. It was better to wait and bide his time. They would get out of this. They had to.

Dayne slowed his breathing. In through his nose, out through his mouth, his chest rising and falling in measured sweeps. He could hear Marlin speaking in his mind. *A panicked mind is a useless one. Take a moment, settle yourself, then watch.*

Three figures stood beside the Dragonguard. One wore a dark hooded mantle, another wore the long black cloak of a Battlemage, while the last was garbed in red and black leather armour, a steel breastplate strapped across their chest.

Besides those three and the Dragonguard, the ship was teeming with imperial soldiers and sailors. The sounds of feet clattering against wood mixed with shouts and commands, all of it fighting against the thumping crash of the waves against the hull of the ship. Two men stood behind Dayne and his parents, their swords drawn. Dayne didn't have to look to know they were there; they hadn't moved since the ship had set sail.

"Are you all right?" Dayne's father whispered, his voice hoarse and tired. He knelt on Dayne's right, blood streaming from a cut above his left eye and his hair matted to his forehead by a mixture of dirt, sweat, and dried gore.

"I'm fine." Dayne gave the slightest of nods. He was tired, his muscles ached, and a litany of fresh cuts laced his body – but he was nowhere near death. "Are you—"

A burst of pain pierced Dayne's head, stars and sunspots flitting across his eyes.

"Keep your mouth shut." The soldier's voice was more akin to a growl than anything else.

Dayne shook his head, attempting to ease the dizziness that had set in from the blow. It was easier said than done with his hands tied behind his back, but he just about managed to keep himself from falling over. He could feel a stream of blood running from the side of his head, down his neck, and into his shirt.

"Get your hands off him!" Dayne's father roared, attempting to get to his feet, only to receive a pommel across the face. Dayne could see the blood drain from the imperial soldier's face when Arkin Ateres barely flinched. The blow was strong enough to draw a stream of blood from Arkin's cheek, but Dayne's father acted as though he had been hit by an angry child. He simply stared at the soldier, his jaw clenched, his eyes cold.

"Easy now, easy now." The voice belonged to the Dragonguard who had taken them in the gardens of Redstone. Her words flowed with an effortless grace, slow and purposeful, as though she were trying to calm a tavern drunk. "You have lost, Lord Ateres. What use is there in causing yourself more pain?"

Dayne lifted his head. The newly forming lump where the soldier had struck him throbbed. Knots of pressure pulsed behind his eyes, causing him to groan. The

Dragonguard stood only a few feet away with each of the three figures at her side.

The man who wore the coat of a Battlemage had the look of someone who had earned that name. His stance was strong, his shoulders were broad, and his eyes looked void of all empathy. A thin scar ran over his right eye, and the bottom half of his face was covered by a close-cut beard. Dayne couldn't help but notice the man's hand constantly tapping on his trouser pocket.

The man in the red and black leathers stood no more than five and a half feet tall, with short blonde hair, two axes hanging from his belt, and an array of knives slotted through a weapons belt that ran over his steel breastplate.

The Dragonguard's eyes fixed on Dayne's father. She looked no older than thirty or forty summers at most, but Dayne knew better. None of the Dragonguard had seen less than four centuries pass before their eyes. It was they who razed the city of Ilnaen, crushed The Order, and brought the continent to its knees. Fane Mortem might sit on the throne in Al'Nasla, but it was the Dragonguard who put him there.

The woman's hair was black as the night sky, her skin a deep brown. Had Dayne not known who and what she was, he would almost have thought her handsome. But he did know, and his blood boiled. She and her dragon had slaughtered tens, maybe hundreds of wyverns. They butchered Thandril. In an instant, Dayne's boiling blood froze, a chill sweeping over him. She was staring straight at him, her eyes so dark they were almost black.

She took a few steps forward until she was almost close enough to touch. "So young," she said, reaching her hand down and tilting Dayne's chin up with her finger. The woman kept her gaze locked on Dayne's for a few moments, her unwavering stare causing the hairs on the back of his neck to stand on end. The corner of her mouth twisted into an almost apologetic smile before she let Dayne's chin drop.

"I was sent here, along with my wing, on personal request from High-Commander Eltoar Daethana. It's not often the Dragonguard are asked to assist in imperial business. Not in a long time." She walked past Dayne's mother, who didn't so much as lift her head. "But you betrayed the graces of Emperor Mortem, and in doing so, you forfeited the lives of every man and woman who died here today. I believe you Valtarans have a saying, do you not? 'By blade and by blood?' How appropriate, for today it was your blades that shed their blood." The woman lifted her arm, pointing toward the city of Stormwatch.

"We will not continue with an imperial boot on our necks!" Dayne's father spat a mixture of saliva and blood onto the deck of the ship, veins pulsing at the side of his head. "The empire takes our children, our food, our way of life. We will never bow down."

"Their blood is on your hands, Arkin." The hooded figure drew down his hood as he spoke. Dayne recognised him immediately as Loren Koraklon, head of House Koraklon – one of the two Houses who had been holding out to pledge their allegiance. *The traitor.*

"Loren!" Rage seethed in Dayne's father's voice as he lifted himself to his feet, only to be struck again by one of the soldiers. He spun, slamming his forehead into the man's nose, blood spurting. Then he went completely rigid, his limbs suspended as though frozen in ice. The sudden look of fear in his father's eyes reminded Dayne that his father could not see what Dayne could: the threads of Air wrapped around his body.

"You're not a smart man, are you?" The Dragonguard tilted her head sideways, an amused laugh escaping her throat. "You must enjoy pain."

"May the gods burn your blood!" Dayne's father shouted at Loren, ignoring the Dragonguard as though she didn't still have him wrapped in threads of Air. "You would betray your own? You are no Valtaran. You are a worm!"

Dayne turned his head, glancing towards his mother who knelt on his right. Despite everything that was happening, she had not said a word. She hadn't even lifted her head. "Mother," he whispered, trying his best not to attract attention. She didn't respond.

"It is you who betrays our people," Loren hissed, stepping forward, his eyes burning with fury. "You cling to the past, desperate for Valtara to bathe in the glory that it once had. And you are willing to throw away Valtaran lives to do it. How many have died here today, Arkin? How many have felt the warm embrace of The Mother years before their time? All you have done is fertilise the soil with the blood of our people. I will not stand by and watch you thrust Valtara into a war it cannot win."

"They died because of *you*!"

"Lies!" Loren lashed out, catching Dayne's father with a sharp strike across the jaw. "The arrogance! Were you not looked after? Did you not have food on your table and gold in your coffers? They died for no reason save your pride and greed."

"Sometimes gold and food aren't enough, Loren. They just aren't enough."

"Silence!" The man in the red and black leathers roared. "We do not have time for this measuring of dicks." He glared at Loren before turning to Dayne's parents, his chest puffed out, his chin raised. "Arkin and Ilya Ateres, my name is Harsted Arnim, commander of the Fifth Army. I am here to inform you that you have been found guilty of treason. You have incited rebellion against the empire and have left us with no choice. You must pay the price, and so must those who stood by you." The man turned to the Dragonguard. "Burn them all."

A sombre expression on her face, the Dragonguard held the man's gaze, a silent exchange passing between them. Neither the Dragonguard nor the commander backed away, cold stares passing between them as though each was challenging the other's authority.

It was the Dragonguard who spoke first, cold fury in her eyes. "So be it."

Dayne's father dropped to the ground, the threads holding him in place evaporating as the Dragonguard turned on her heels, muttering as she walked back towards the bow of the ship, the others following in tow.

"No. No! Loren, don't let them do this!" Dayne's father's voice cracked as he screamed, pleading. Dayne had never heard his father beg. Not once in his life. "These are your people! Do *not* do this. Whatever you think of me, this is not the answer. Your soul will never be clean."

Loren hesitated for a moment, his gaze tracking the wooden boards of the deck, shadows covering most of his face. But then, with one last look towards Dayne's father, he turned and joined the others at the bow, the boards creaking beneath him.

Before Dayne could ask what was happening a blood-chilling roar erupted overhead, followed by a gust of wind so powerful it seemed to pull at the air, almost knocking Dayne to the deck. For a brief moment, the pale light of the moon disappeared, swallowed by a shape that flew low overhead, shrouding the world in darkness. *Dragon.*

"No!" Dayne's father leapt to his feet once more, deftly avoiding another pommel strike from the soldier who thought to teach him a lesson. His hands still tied behind his back, Arkin Ateres slammed his forehead into the soldier's face before knocking him overboard with a shoulder charge. The other soldiers moved to restrain Dayne's father, but every soul on the ship stopped as the first roar was met by two others, and the sky lit up as though lightning had spewed from the clouds above.

But it wasn't lightning. It was dragonfire. Three flowing columns of flame that poured down over the fortress city, crashing against the walls in breaking waves of orange and red. Again and again the dragons dove, bathing the city in fire. Screams filled the air, echoing down the cliff, rolling over the water's surface. Cries of men and women as their skin melted from their bones. The spluttering moans of the dying as they choked on dust and ash. The wails of children as the fortress was slowly turned into an oven, and they were cooked alive.

Dayne's father dropped to his knees, his shoulders slumping. "No… *please* no…"

Tears streamed down Dayne's face. His heart twisted in his chest. "Why would anyone do this?"

Dayne turned to his mother. Her eyes were open now, her head lifted. Tears had carved paths through the dirt and blood that coated her face; claw marks of sorrow. Dayne could see the twitch in her jaw as she ground her teeth, her stare fixed on those who stood at the bow of the ship.

After a few moments, she shifted her gaze, turning to Dayne. Her eyes were red and raw from crying, but within them Dayne saw two things clear as day: insurmountable loss and pure fury.

"Be ready to run," she whispered, her eyes still locked on his, her voice barely audible against the screams of the dying and the crashing of the waves.

"But, I—"

"Dayne, be quiet and listen. Run for the rail, and jump. Swim back to shore. Find Alina and Baren. Take them to the farm at Myrefall. Keep them safe."

"But… No, I can't leave you."

The slightest hint of a smile touched the corner of his mother's mouth, and then it was gone. She touched her forehead to his. "You, your brothers, and your sister are the best things I ever did with my life. Look after each other, Dayne."

"I—"

"Shut up." One of the soldiers barked.

"Do as I say," Dayne's mother continued, ignoring the soldier.

Dayne nodded, not breaking from his mother's gaze. "I love you."

"Oi! I said shut the fuck up!" The soldier reached down, tugging at Ilya's shoulder.

"I will never stop loving you, my son." It was only at that moment Dayne realised his mother's hands were no longer bound. Cut ropes lay on the deck beside her, a glint of steel flashed in her hand. She reached behind him, slicing through his bonds, then held his gaze for only a fraction of a moment before turning.

"Get back on your—" The soldier's voice cut out as Ilya rose to her feet and rammed her long, thin blade through his eye, blood sluicing from the wound. Dayne recognised the blade in an instant. It was the one his mother always strapped to the inside of her thigh. *"You can never have too many blades,"* he remembered her saying to him on more than one occasion. *"And most men have too much decency to check a woman's thigh. The ones that don't? Well, they're only more reason for the blade to exist."*

Leaving the blade embedded in the man's skull, Ilya pried his sword free from his hands as he collapsed to the deck, his body limp and lifeless. Using her own momentum to carry her forward, she spun, avoiding the swing of a second imperial soldier, slicing through the ribs of another.

"Father!" Dayne roared.

All it took was a glance, and Arkin Ateres rose to his feet, charging into the soldiers who attacked Ilya, sending them sprawling to the deck, and freeing his bound hands on a soldier's blade.

"Dayne, run!" Dayne's mother screamed, sliding her sword across a soldier's throat before ramming the pommel into another woman's cheek.

Holding his fear at bay, Dayne lifted himself to his feet, his body aching, joints stiff. The sores around his wrists pulled and tore, blood trickling into his palms. His head wanted him to do as his mother had told him – urged him to run. But it wasn't that simple. His heart twisted as he watched his mother and father fight tooth and nail. For every blade that touched their skin, two soldiers fell, then two more.

"Dayne, ru—" Blood trickled over Arkin's lip as his eyes met Dayne's. His hands dropped to his chest, where a long steel blade had punched through his sternum.

"No!" Dayne screamed, taking a step towards his parents.

His father dropped to his knees as the blade was pulled free. He clasped his hands to his chest, trying desperately to stem the flow of blood that seeped through his fingers. The light in his eyes fading, he collapsed on his side, his chest rapidly rising and falling, desperately dragging in his last breaths of air.

In his father's place stood the Dragonguard. Blood ran down the length of the woman's sword, pooling at the tip, dripping onto Dayne's father's now lifeless body.

Something inside Dayne snapped. He charged, reaching out to the Spark, feeling its warmth calling to him. This woman would die. Her ribs would cave in and crush her black heart. Her skin would peel from her body.

Just as Dayne began to pull on the threads of Earth, Water, and Spirit, something slammed into him, knocking him off balance, sending him crashing to the ground. The force threw him down, pinning him in place. He tried to move, tried to thrash his arms and legs, but nothing worked. He was trapped. *How is she doing this?*

As though the woman had read his thoughts, whatever force had been pinning him lifted him, pulling him into the air like strings dragging a puppet.

The Dragonguard stood before him, a glowing, red gemstone in one hand, her sword in the other. Dayne's mother knelt at her feet, likely held by the same force that suspended Dayne in the air. Blood streamed from the many cuts that laced her body, and the muscle and tissue surrounding her left eye had swollen to the size of an orange.

"What do we do with you?" the Dragonguard said, tilting her head sideways as she ran her gaze over Dayne.

"He must die," Loren said, stepping forward, his jaw set, his brow furrowed. "We can control the younger two, but this one cannot live."

"No!" Dayne's mother shouted, the struggle evident on her face as she pushed against the invisible bonds that held her.

"You don't like that idea then?" the Dragonguard said, slowly making her way around so she stood between Dayne and his mother. The Battlemage and the Lorian commander moved with her, standing only a foot or so away. Loren stood opposite, inches from Dayne's father's body.

Out of the corner of his eye, Dayne noticed the Battlemage staring at him, the man's green eyes piercing right through him.

"Spare him, please."

The Dragonguard knelt, resting the tip of her blade against the deck of the ship, her eyes level with Dayne's mother's. For a long moment they just stared at each other, but then the woman spoke. "Rakina"—She turned her head, looking towards the Battlemage who stood a foot or so away, his cloak billowing in the ocean wind—"will you allow fate to choose?"

Silence. Then, the Battlemage nodded, slipped his hand into his trouser pocket, and produced a thick, golden coin.

"What is this? You can't be serious." Loren stepped forward, his hand grasped around the pommel of his sword.

"If you take one step closer," the Battlemage said, shifting his gaze to Loren, "I will gut you like a pig."

Dayne could see the look of hesitation on Loren's face. Four black rings bisected by a thick black line were inked on Loren's left forearm, accompanied by two rings on his left arm. The man was a blademaster. One of the most renowned in all Valtara. But this *Rakina* was a Battlemage. Loren would be dead before he could draw his sword.

In the end, Loren didn't move another inch. He clenched his jaw and glared, his hand not straying from the pommel of his sword.

"Good boy." A satisfied smile spread across the Battlemage's face. He flicked the coin into the air, the sound of its movements masked by the crashing of the waves and the creaking of the ship.

But to Dayne, those sounds yielded to the thundering beat of his heart as the golden coin flipped through the air. Tears streamed down his mother's face, her eyes never leaving his. Kneeling there, battered and bleeding, she mouthed the words, "I love you."

The coin landed soundlessly in the Battlemage's outstretched hand. He took one look, then gave a short nod. "The boy lives."

The invisible bonds that held Dayne disappeared, fading from existence as though they never were. He dropped to the deck, stumbling slightly as his feet connected with the wood. Relief flooded his body, an icy river filling his veins, washing over his skin. He could hear Loren shouting, fury in his voice. But Dayne didn't look at the head of House Koraklon. He looked at his mother, allowing their shared relief to bring a fleeting moment of happiness.

"Your wish is granted, Ilya of House Ateres." Moving as she spoke, the Dragonguard swung her blade. Dayne's heart twisted, and a hollow formed in his chest as the steel sliced through his mother's neck and took her head from her shoulders.

"No! No! Mother!" He leaped forward, every hair on his body tingling, numbness smothering his mind. A hand clapped him in the chest, shoving him back.

"She had to die." It was the Battlemage, the one the Dragonguard had called Rakina. "Don't be stupid."

"I'll kill you!" Dayne screamed. Not at the Battlemage, but at all of them. His throat burned as he roared, the numbness being supplanted by soul-rending pain. He had broken bones and taken steel, but those wounds were nothing.

"No, you won't, boy." The invisible force returned, wrapping around his body, tethering him in place. The Dragonguard stood beside the Battlemage, the red gemstone in her hand glowing with renewed vigour. "You are hereby banished from these lands by order of both the Dragonguard and the Lorian Empire. Should you return, you will hang in the central plaza of Skyfell. Your sister and brother will watch your neck break, and then they will be hung with the same noose. I will personally strip your bloodline from this world. Your life is spared by the grace of The Saviour and the will of fate. You are now, and will forever remain, an exile."

With that, she turned, the invisible bonds fading as she walked away.

An uncontrollable shiver set itself in Dayne's bones. His chest trembled, a tremor ran through his hands, and his legs felt like reeds in the wind. He wasn't cold; he was empty. The sight of his father's and mother's bodies, their blood seeping into wood of the deck, turned his stomach. Tears burned his eyes, streaking down his cheeks and dripping off his chin. Slowly, in the dark caverns of his empty soul, a fire ignited. His fingers twisted into a fist and his chest heaved. He reached out to the Spark.

"Don't be an idiot." The Battlemage stepped in front of Dayne, their eyes locked.

Startled, Dayne let go of the Spark. If any of them found out he could wield the Spark, he wouldn't leave that boat alive. The empire was ruthless when it came to any mages who had slipped through their 'testing' as children. Dayne had seen enough men and women hung to know that to be true.

"Fate gave you a second chance. Don't waste it."

Before Dayne could even think, the man reached out to the Spark, pulled in threads of Air, and rammed them into Dayne's chest.

Dayne careened backwards, slamming into the rail of the ship, the force of the threads launching him over the edge. In seconds, the icy embrace of the water swept over him as he broke the surface and plunged into the ocean.

Every muscle in Dayne's body burned, screaming at him to stop. He reached up, resting his forearm on the rock-face to his left. His salt-crusted skin cracked with every movement. His legs were raw and chafed. It had taken him an hour or so to swim back to the Abaddian cliffs upon which Redstone stood. Alina, Baren, and Marlin hadn't been in the caves when Dayne had gotten there. They must have been forced to move on.

He needed to keep looking.

Turning so the flat of his back pressed against the rock, Dayne looked out over the ocean, shifting his gaze to Stormwatch. He felt a stomach-churning weightlessness at the sight of the blazing inferno. Dayne clenched his jaw, forcing the tears down. The flames might still be raging, but anyone left within the city was no longer drawing breath. He could mourn later.

"Alina," he whispered as he reached the familiar cave mouth that sat into the cliff. From the ocean, the cave would barely have been visible, but Dayne knew better. Decades before the rebellion, his great-great-grandfather had a passage constructed behind a bookcase in his study in Redstone, leading to the cave mouth that now stood before Dayne. "Baren? Marlin?"

The cave was empty.

"Please be all right. By the light of Varyn," Dayne whispered.

Dayne allowed himself a few moments of rest before making his way through the cave and into the darkness of the chamber on the other side. His father always kept a torch wrapped in a fat-soaked rag sitting in a sconce in the chamber. But Dayne had no means of lighting it, and he dared not use the Spark lest any nearby imperial mages sense him. Instead, he reached out with his fingertips, running them against the walls to find his way in the darkness. Putting one foot in front of the other, he stepped into the tunnel that led from the chamber and climbed the staircase to his father's office, dust and dirt crunching beneath his bare feet. By the time he felt the touch of wood, his brow was slicked with sweat, and his legs burned with renewed vigour.

Drawing a deep breath, Dayne pressed his ear against the wood of the bookcase that covered the entrance to the tunnel. He listened for any sounds on the other side, any subtle vibrations or voices. Once he was reasonably sure the room was empty, he reached down and undid the latch that held the bookcase in place.

Eerie silence greeted him as the hidden doorway slid open, and he stepped into his father's study. It looked just the same as it had earlier that night. Not a single thing was out of place. Part of him expected his father to stroll through the door at any moment. But that wouldn't happen. He would never see his father again.

He would never feel his mother's embrace or hear the sweet sound of her voice. Those things were gone now. Dayne cast a mournful glance over the study, running his hand along the top of the leather couch nearest to him, before setting off down the hall. He needed to get to his chambers, gather supplies, and find Alina, Baren, and Mera.

Dayne kept to the shadows as he moved through the keep. The hallways were mostly empty except for the occasional patrol of Lorian soldiers, sharp steel in their fists. But even those patrols were few and far between. Most of the soldiers must have still been fighting in the streets, just enough left behind to hold Redstone. By the time Dayne reached his chambers, his heart was beating out of his chest, sweat slicking his brow.

No candles were alight in the room. The only source of illumination was the glow of the moon as it washed in through the window by the bed, bathing the stone in a cold white.

Moving as quickly as he could, Dayne set about gathering anything he might need. Sitting atop his bed was a slightly worn leather satchel his mother had given him when he saw his sixteenth summer. The finest of Valtaran leather, made from the hide of the Andruvin Deer of the Rolling Mountains. He sighed as he ran his hands over the smooth leather, then undid the brass buckle, tossing in a waterskin, a length of rope, a blanket, firestarter, an inkwell, and a pen. His touch lingered on the well-worn edges of a leatherbound book that sat by his bedside – another present from his mother. He tossed it into the bag.

Once the satchel was full, he slung it over his shoulder and pulled his weapons belt from the chest in the corner of the room, buckling it around his hip, sliding his sword and knives into place.

Lightning jolted him at the sound of the door creaking open. He leapt into motion. Ripping a knife from his belt, he darted for the door, reaching out and clasping his left hand over the intruder's mouth, holding the man up against the wall with the blade of the knife pressed against his neck.

"Don't say a word," Dayne whispered, squinting in the dim moonlight. As his eyes adjusted, he realised it wasn't a man he held against the wall, but a boy. One he recognised. "Iloen, it's me, Dayne."

The boy gulped, his eyes widening as he examined Dayne's face.

"I'm going to let you go now. Stay quiet."

The boy nodded.

Dayne pulled his hand from over Iloen's mouth then closed the door, sliding his knife back into place. "Are you all right?"

Iloen nodded again. The boy had seen no more than twelve summers, the same as Alina. He worked as a porter in the kitchens with his mother, Sora. His father, Aren, was one of the Redstone guard – Dayne knew them well. "What are you doing here, Iloen? It's not safe. You need to stay in your quarters."

No sooner had the words left Dayne's mouth than Iloen began to sob, holding his hand over his nose and mouth. "My mother… she…" The boy shook his head, trying his best to stifle his sobs. "I was looking for my father when I saw you leaving your father's study, my lord. I heard you were dead."

Dayne lowered himself to one knee so his eyes were level with Iloen's. "It's all right," he whispered, placing his hand on Iloen's shoulder. Dayne knew his words were lies. The likelihood was that Aren was dead, and judging by the tears that streamed down Iloen's face, so was Sora. "I need you to be strong for me, Iloen. Do you understand?"

Iloen nodded, sniffling as he tried to regain composure.

"Good lad. Now, have you seen my sister, or my brother? Alina and Baren."

Iloen shook his head. "No, my lord. Not since this morning. But the soldiers have been looking for them for hours. I could hear them shouting."

"What of Mera? You know Mera, don't you? The beautiful lady with bright blue eyes."

"I… I'm not sure."

"Come on Iloen, you know her. You watched her put me on my back not two weeks gone, in the training yard."

Iloen's eyes lit up. "I do know her!"

Of course, that's how he remembers. "Good. This is very important, Iloen. Have you seen her? Do you know if she's all right?"

Iloen nodded, a brightness returning to his eyes. "I did! She and the others were locked in their chambers when the soldiers came. Some died…" Iloen's voice trailed off for a moment. "But Mera didn't. I'm sure of it!"

A wave of relief washed over Dayne, a weightless knot twisting in his stomach. "Thank you, Iloen. Thank you."

Dayne clasped his hands down on the boy's shoulders. "All right, you can't stay here. It's not safe. I need you to go back to your quarters. Stay there until someone comes for you."

"But I want to stay with you, I—"

"Iloen, I need you to do what I say." Dayne pulled a knife from his belt and pushed it into Iloen's hands. "Take this. Hopefully you won't need it."

"Y-yes, my lord," the boy stuttered.

"All right. Go now, and be quick about it. Don't let anyone see you." As Iloen turned, another thought touched Dayne's mind. What if he couldn't find Baren or Alina? "Iloen, if you see Baren or Alina, tell them I survived. Tell them I will come for them."

"Yes, my lord. I promise." Iloen nodded before stepping out of the room and darting off down the hallway.

Dayne hated himself for letting Iloen go on his own, but the boy was quick, and Dayne simply didn't have the time.

He stripped off his salt-crusted clothes, replacing them with a fresh tunic, trousers, and a pair of sandals, then crept from the room.

If Alina and Baren were not in the cave, and if the empire hadn't found them yet, then Marlin had likely taken them and made for the farm at Myrefall. That's where Dayne needed to go. He would take the passage in his father's office. But first, he needed to find Mera.

Even with the keep teeming with Lorian soldiers, it wasn't long before Dayne found himself at the doors to Mera's chambers. As his palm rested against the rough grain of the wood, he heard sobs from within.

"It's all right, Mera," Dayne heard Mera's mother, Aeyrin, say.

"If anything happens to him, Mother…"

Hearing Mera's voice caused Dayne's breath to catch in his throat. A slight tremble set into his hand as he pressed his fingers against the door. All he wanted to do was push open that door, wrap his arms around Mera, and never let go. He wanted to feel the comfort of her touch as he wept and the love of her heart as she held him. But he knew that if he walked through that door, he would be damning her to the same fate as his own. He couldn't stay in Valtara. If the empire found him, he'd be strung up by a noose, and Mera would never let him leave alone; he knew that in his heart.

Dayne rested his forehead against the wooden door, letting out a sigh, tears burning at the corners of his eyes. "I can't do that to you," he whispered. His chest ached as though his ribs were closing in around his heart. Dayne drew in a deep breath, closing his eyes as he did, then let it out slowly. "I love you, Mera." He spoke the words as though she could hear him. "I'm sorry."

Dayne lifted his palm from the door and stepped back. It took every ounce of strength within him to walk away. Each step like a knife stabbing at his chest. But he kept walking. Forcing himself to put one foot in front of the other. *I'll come back. I promise.*

He made his way back through the keep, sticking to the shadows, taking the servants' passageways and narrowly avoiding at least three patrols. It wasn't long before he, once again, found himself standing before the large, stained doors to his father's study, his gaze resting on a rough-cut groove that sat below the topmost brass hinge on the left door. He had only been a child when he had made that groove. Marlin had set him to a week in the orchard because of it, but his mother had simply complimented him on his strength. To say that Dayne would miss her would be the gravest of understatements. For a parent is to a child what sun is to a flower.

Letting out a suppressed sigh, Dayne pushed open the door, only just enough for him to slip through, closing it behind him.

"Something in your eyes told me you wouldn't leave so easily."

Dayne froze, the air catching in his lungs, his muscles tensing.

The Dragonguard stood with her back to him, her dark hair blowing gently in the breeze, her white plate armour glistening as she looked out the window behind his father's desk. "I admire it, truly." The woman turned to face Dayne, her hands spread out, her sword strapped to her hip. "Tonight was not something I *wanted* to do. My hand was forced."

The sound of metal on stone alerted Dayne to the presence of two Lorian soldiers standing either side of the doors, their hands resting on the pommels of their swords.

This is my chance. She's right there.

Three couches and Dayne's father's desk stood between him and the Dragonguard. The couches occupied the centre of the study, two facing each other, with the third facing away from Dayne.

Dayne pulled two knives from his belt and leaped, the sound of metal boots following behind him. He kicked off the back of the couch and dropped to the ground on the other side, twisting and driving a knife through the skull of the soldier who was scrambling after him. Leaving the knife wedged in the man's skull, Dayne shoved him backwards into his companion, sending them both sprawling to the floor. He turned to face the Dragonguard, drawing his sword as he did.

"Oh, the arrogance of youth." Dayne felt the woman reach out to the Spark, and then he was lifted off his feet, careening through the room, thick threads of Air wrapped around him. He gasped for breath, his throat slamming into the Dragonguard's outstretched hand, his sword skittering off the stone as it was pulled from his grasp.

He tried to move, tried to slip a knife from his belt, but his limbs wouldn't obey; the Dragonguard had pinned them in place with threads of Air. He reached out to the Spark, desperate, pulling with everything he had. But he found nothing.

"Did you really think I had not sensed you on the ship? I felt you the moment you reached for the Spark, but I am no Inquisitor. I am not part of their Circle, and I do not subscribe to their beliefs. If Fane wants the empire to round up all those who can touch the Spark, that is his business, but it is not ours."

The Dragonguard released her hold on Dayne's throat.

"Do not mistake this for weakness." The Dragonguard reached into a pouch tied to her weapons belt, producing a pendant on a leather string, a gleaming sapphire bound with gold – Alina's pendant.

"Alina…" The word left Dayne's mouth of its own volition.

"She is alive," the woman said, holding the pendant in front of Dayne for a few moments before placing it back into the pouch. "We found them an hour or so ago, huddled in a cave at the base of the cliffs. Their guardian fought well. I spared him." Dayne felt himself being lowered to the ground, his feet touching the stone, his eyes drawing level with the Dragonguard's.

"I need you to understand me, Dayne Ateres. Think of me what you will. I am a woman of my word. Before I took your mother's head, I promised her I would let you and your siblings live. But I also swore that you were to be exiled, and should you step foot in these lands again, I would erase your bloodline."

Dayne struggled against the threads that held him, fire burning in his veins. "If you touch a hair on their heads, I'll—"

"You'll what?" The woman stepped closer to Dayne, close enough that he could feel her breath on his skin. Her gaze pierced him. She shook her head, stepping away. "They will be raised under the tutelage of your steward to lead House Ateres."

"As pawns!"

"Yes," the Dragonguard said, her tone flat. "As pawns, but alive. No harm will come to them so long as you stay away. You have my word."

"Your word means nothing! Why should I trust your word?" Fury seared Dayne's body, his head pounding, his jaw clenched. She was so close.

"Because I kept my word to your mother. I let you live."

The threads of Air that were wrapped around Dayne's body pulled tighter, and then he was moving, hurtling towards the open window. The cool rush of air hit him, the threads evaporating around him. He looked back, glimpsing the Dragonguard standing in the window. And then he was falling.

Pure terror blended seamlessly with an odd sense of calm as the rockface of the Abaddian cliffs flashed passed him. His pulse quickened, a sense of weightlessness overcoming him. He drew in a deep breath, letting his body relax, then he reached out to the Spark, drawing on threads of Air and Water, bracing himself.

I will come back for you.

PART 2

AN EYE FOR AN EYE

TWO YEARS LATER

III

Vengeance

Winter's Keep, Loria
Year 3070 after doom

Dayne swirled the blood and saliva in his mouth, then spat it out, watching it mix with the dust on the floor of the cell.

Crack. The soldier slammed his fist into Dayne's jaw again, calling forth more streams of blood, teeth slicing the tender flesh on the inside of his cheek.

Dayne stood in a large stone cell fronted by latticed bars of iron, steel manacles locked around his wrists and linked by a chain that ran through a loop on the wall. The cell itself was attached to a long corridor that connected to precisely forty-seven other cells just like the one in which Dayne currently resided. Not a single cell was empty; some housed as many as nine or ten souls. From what Dayne had heard, the dungeons of Winter's Keep were rarely empty.

It had taken him two years to track down Harsted Arnim – the only name he had been given that night. *"Burn them all."* The words that had set a city on fire were etched into Dayne's memory. But even more than that, Harsted Arnim was the only one he knew who could give him the name of the Dragonguard. So many times, he had thought the commander to be within his grasp, and so many times he had been wrong. Tracking down the man was like chasing a ghost. And so, once Dayne had heard rumour Harsted Arnim would be in Winter's Keep that night – the same night Dayne had entered the city – he had no choice but to find a way into the keep itself. And that was where he now found himself.

Winter's Keep, named after the city in which it resided, was renowned as an impregnable fortress. Manned day and night. Hundred-foot-high smooth walls, near impossible to scale. Illuminated by brazier light wherever shadows lingered. Being taken to the dungeons seemed the simplest way of gaining entry, though he regretted his plan more and more with every hit to the face.

Two Lorian soldiers stood in the cell with Dayne, both garbed in the red and black leathers of the Lorian army. One was the stocky young man who was trying his best to break his knuckles on Dayne's face. He couldn't have seen more than eighteen summers. He stunk of ale, and his eyes were sunken from a lack of sleep. His dark hair was slicked back, oiled and combed with meticulous care.

The second was a middle-aged woman with raven-black hair and an unwrinkled face that said she didn't laugh much. She stood by the open cell door, her eyes narrowed as she watched the younger man 'interrogate' Dayne. She had been there, at the inn, when the fighting had started – thrown a good punch or two as well. Though the cut under her left eye looked like it would have a black and yellow bruise to accompany it in the morning.

"You're not so tough now, are you?" The young man said, his chest heaving, sweat dripping from his brow. Thin streams of blood ran from cuts on his knuckles.

The woman snorted, shaking her head. "He's chained to the wall, Gar. And you're hurting yourself more than you're hurting him."

The younger man turned sharply, fury in his eyes. He moved to within inches of the woman's face, his gaze level with hers.

"Down, boy." The woman didn't so much as flinch. She returned Gar's stare, daring him to do something.

"Has he said anything else?" The tension in the cell vanished at the sound of a third voice, replaced by something entirely different – fear. Dayne turned his head, blinking blood from his eyes. The man who had entered the cell wore at least fifty summers' worth of wrinkles on his face. He was gangly with razor-sharp features, his dark hair greying at the sides. He was tall, garbed in black leathers with a steel breastplate strapped across his chest, a sword belted to his left hip, two knives at his right – angled slightly forward – and a third knife in his boot, the tip of the handle poking out. This man was a killer. Dayne could smell it off him.

"No… Captain," the younger soldier stuttered, stepping backwards, his voice sheepish.

The older man raised an eyebrow towards the woman.

She shook her head. "Just keeps saying the same thing he said at the inn – 'Take me to Harsted Arnim'. We're wasting our time."

The older man nodded, running his tongue along his teeth and clasping his hands behind his back. He stopped in front of Dayne, clicking his tongue against the roof of his mouth, then crossing his arms. "You put five soldiers in the infirmary, along with six patrons." The man held Dayne's gaze, watching him, measuring him. "The only reason you weren't gutted and tossed in a ditch was because you knew Harsted Arnim's name. If you won't talk, there's no reason to keep you alive."

Dayne returned the captain's stare.

After a long moment, the man spoke again. "What business have you with the commander of the Fifth Army?"

Dayne must have struck a nerve. They were very eager to know whatever it was that he knew – which was very little, but they didn't know that.

"Take me to Harsted Arnim."

"What makes you think he is here?"

"Take me to—"

An elbow to the face knocked Dayne backwards, cutting his sentence short. Stars burst across his vision, and he was pretty sure he felt a tooth come loose. The coppery tang of fresh blood coated his tongue. Spitting the blood onto the ground, he turned back and met the captain's stare once more, unblinking.

"You're a tough son of a bitch," the captain said, his eyes narrowing as he stared at Dayne. "Or at least you think you are. But I have people here who would jump at the chance to help you find your tongue, and then they would set it on fire in front of you. I think it's about time I let one of them have their chance."

I should have just tried to climb the walls.

"Sir," Gar said, rubbing the cuts on his right hand. "Why are we even bothering? Let's just get rid of him."

The older man glared at Gar, his gaze boring through the young soldier. "Because," the man growled, wrapping his fingers through Dayne's hair and pulling his head back, "he knows names he has no right to know. People don't just start brawls then surrender and start calling to be brought to see the commander of the Fifth Army."

"But should we not just tell the commander?" the young soldier asked. "He should be finishing up his meeting with Lord Gurning soon, I'm sure we can—"

"Shut your mouth!" The woman clapped the younger soldier on the back of the head, but she was too late. Dayne had heard what he needed to know. *He is here. Finally.*

Reaching out to the Spark, Dayne pulled at threads of Air, working them through the locks of the shackles. Within seconds, the shackles were off. But before they even reached the ground, Dayne lunged forward. He wrapped a thin thread of Air around the knife in the older man's boot and pulled it upward, sending the blade slicing through the man's right hand as he reached for his sword.

Ignoring the man's howls, Dayne used more threads of Air to pull another knife from its place on the man's hip. His hand met the knife in mid-air, his fingers wrapping around the handle. He drove the blade down into the top of the man's skull. Flesh gave way to bone, then the resistance faded and the blade plunged to the hilt. Recognition flashed across the man's eyes before they rolled to the back of his head, then the blade slid free and he dropped to the ground.

The woman charged Dayne, ripping her sword free from its scabbard.

Turning to face the charge, Dayne shifted his weight to his back foot, lifted his right leg, and caught her square in the chest with the flat of his foot. The force of the strike sent her crashing to the ground like a sack of stones, her sword clattering beside her. Without hesitating, Dayne lifted his leg once more and brought his full weight down on the woman's leg, feeling her shin bone hold for a moment before snapping like the branch of a tree. The woman looked as though she were going to scream, but then she went limp, her shoulders slumped, and her head dangled forward. Shock must have taken her.

The shifting of feet to his right caught Dayne's attention. He bent over and leaned in, catching the younger soldier, Gar, across the legs. Rising to his full height, Dayne launched Gar over his back and into the stone wall on the other side of the cell.

The soldier tried to drag himself to his feet, but Dayne was faster. He cleared the distance between the two of them and drove his foot into the side of the young man's head with as much force as he could muster. There was a slight *cracking* sound, and Gar dropped onto the flat of his belly. He didn't move.

Dayne turned back to the semi-conscious woman, who lay groaning on the floor. Reaching down, he grabbed her by the scruff of her neck and dragged her along the ground, pressing her against the iron bars of the cell. "Tell me where Harsted Arnim is."

"I ain't telling you shit." The woman's head drooped left and right as she spoke, her words sounding like they came from the mouth of someone who had been drinking ale for days.

Clamping his hand over her mouth, Dayne drove the knife into her flesh just below her collarbone then dragged it downward, blood pouring from the wound. The vibrations of her muffled screams rippled against the skin of his palm. He looked her in the eye. "Speak."

"My leg… I… I'm not… telling you—"

Dayne clamped his hand back over her mouth and twisted the blade, pulling it out before jamming it down to the hilt. He kept his eyes locked on hers. "The longer you make me wait, the more pain you will endure. I will break more than your leg. You have my word."

The woman grimaced as the blade twisted a little, but she kept her mouth shut.

"This was your choice," Dayne whispered, staring into the woman's eyes. He didn't want to do any of this. But he would die before he let anything, or anyone, get in his way. He would do what he had to.

Letting go of the knife, his other hand still holding the neck of the woman's armour, he reached down and placed his palm against the cool leather that protected the woman's side. Warmth flowed through him as he pulled on thin threads of Fire, channelling them through his palm and into the leather. "You should feel the heat by now," he said, holding the woman's stare. "First, the leather will begin to blacken and char, clinging to your body. But it won't burn easy, leather never does. It will get hotter and hotter until your skin begins to bubble and blister, the smell of your own burning flesh filling your nostrils. Eventually, it will feel like you are being set on fire from the inside out."

Just like your people did to mine.

The woman's eyes widened. For a moment Dayne thought she would break, but then her determined glare returned.

"So be it."

Dayne pulled harder on the threads, feeling the power surge through him. He wrapped threads of Air around the woman's mouth to quieten her screaming. The smell of burning leather and charred flesh filled the air almost instantly, coating the back of Dayne's throat with a horrid layer of thick smoke. He kept pushing, feeling the Fire flow through him. The empire had burned his people. He would do the same in return. *Burn them all.*

One. Two. Three. Four. Five.

Dayne released the threads of Fire, letting the heat fade away. He pulled his hand from the woman's side to inspect the mottled mess of oozing black. Lifting his head, he studied her face. Tears streamed down her face, and her eyes were red and raw. Her lips were moving, but no sound escaped. Slowly, he removed the wrap of Air from around her mouth.

Almost as soon as he did, the woman began to scream. He immediately replaced the threads, silencing her once more. "Quietly, or it all starts again."

Dayne pulled back the threads of air that covered her mouth.

"Please…" she sobbed, her body shaking. "No more."

"Where is Harsted Arnim?"

"He's in…" The woman's voice trailed off for a moment, hesitation creeping in.

"Is he someone worth dying for?"

The woman held Dayne's gaze. Then he saw something flash across her eyes: resignation. "He's in Lord Gurning's drawing room"—She grunted, wincing in pain—"on the fourth floor."

"How do I get there?"

"There's a servants' stairwell down the hallway, outside the door. The stairwell comes out right beside the drawing room. It's the double doors gilded with a lion."

Dayne nodded. "Thank you," he said, releasing his hold on the woman. "I can't risk you screaming. May The Mother embrace you."

Before the soldier could react, Dayne pulled the knife from her shoulder and drove it into the side of her head. A pang of guilt pulled at his heart. *I will do whatever needs to be done.*

Letting the woman's body slump sideways, Dayne moved to the younger soldier. He shoved the man onto his back then proceeded to strip him of his armour and sword. *It will be a tight fit, but it'll have to do.*

It didn't take long to find the servants' stairwell down the hall from the dungeons. Dayne counted each step as he ascended – an old habit he'd had since he was a child. The leather armour chafed, but it was as good a fit as he could have hoped for. He dropped his hand to the belt he had taken from the dead soldier, his fingers brushing off the hilts of the two knives that sat at his hip then over the pommel of the sword. He needed to be ready.

His heart pounded in his ears, knots twisted in his stomach, and the slightest of trembles set into his hand. Two years, and he had never come this close. He would not fail. Either Harsted Arnim would die tonight, or Dayne would.

Servants in red and black livery passed Dayne as he darted up the stairwell. They threw sideways glances in his direction – likely curious as to why a soldier was running up the stairs, his face laced with cuts and bruises, blood dripping from his nose – but none dared stop and question him. He didn't suppose it was ever commonplace for a servant to even look twice at a soldier.

Once he reached the fourth floor, Dayne stopped for a moment and took a deep breath before stepping out of the stairwell. The hallway was easily twenty feet wide, a stone banister along its edge, overlooking the floor below, and a long white and gold carpet that ran along its centre – at least, he could tell the carpet used to be white and gold. Now it looked more like a murky grey and tarnished yellow, marred by the footprints of time. Small, oil-burning lamps were set sparsely in alcoves along the wall, washing the hallway in a dim, orange light. About fifty feet to the left, Dayne saw what he had come for: a large set of wooden double doors with a golden lion emblazoned across their front.

Two soldiers in heavy steel plate stood in front of the doors, their backs straight, swords at their hips. The five stars on their breastplates marked them as soldiers of the Fifth Army. Dayne's pulse quickened. *He really is here.* All traces of nerves and fear flooded from his body, replaced by a cold certainty. *He will die today, and I will get the name I have come for.*

Checking the knives at his belt once more, Dayne walked towards the guards, allowing a heavy limp to creep into his step. The cuts and blood would help him here. "Please, help," he called out as he let himself stumble sideways, grasping onto the banister.

The sound of armoured footsteps told him that the soldiers had taken the bait.

"What's happened?" one of the guards called out as they rushed towards him.

"There's been an attack," Dayne answered, pushing himself away from the banister and letting himself fall forward so the soldier would catch him.

As Dayne fell into the soldier's outstretched arms, he reached up, clasping his hand over the man's mouth. Then, in a flash of movement, he slipped a knife from his belt and drove it up into the soldier's neck, using the man's own body to shield the attack from the other soldier, letting the blood flow down over his chest. Tossing the dying man to the floor, Dayne launched the knife through the air, charging after it as the blade sunk into the second soldier's eye. The man stumbled sideways, then dropped, Dayne catching him just before he hit the floor. Blood spilled over Dayne's hands he lowered the man gently to the stone. There was no need to attract any more attention.

Dayne looked over the scene, the two men lying in pools of their own blood, their lives cut short for his vengeance. *Harden yourself. More blood needs be spilt, and more again.*

Taking a deep breath, Dayne leaned down and pulled the knife from the soldier's eye, wiping the blood on the man's trousers. Standing back to his full height, he walked to the set of large double doors that marked the drawing room of Lord Gurning. The place where he would finally find Harsted Arnim – the man who ordered the burning of Stormshold. The man whose blood would coat the stone of Winter's Keep.

Leaning forward, Dayne placed a hand on each of the double doors, the steel of the knife in his right fist clinking slightly against the gilding on the large lion's side. A tremble took hold of his chest. Sweat mixed with the blood on his face, painting his lips with a salty iron tang. *Finally.*

With one giant heave, he swung the doors open.

The drawing room was enormous. Easily a hundred feet long and at least eighty feet across. Windows adorned with white and gold curtains were set into the long, stone wall opposite Dayne. Candles sat in sweeping cast iron chandeliers overhead, their light mingling with that of the crackling fireplace on the right side of the room. Directly across from Dayne, a large open archway framed by the same white and gold curtains as the windows led out to a semi-circular balcony rimmed by a high stone balustrade. Two figures stood on the balcony. One was tall with broad shoulders and a receding hairline, garbed in a formal red doublet. The other stood nearly two full heads shorter, dressed in full leathers, with blonde hair, and two axes hanging from his belt. *Harsted Arnim.*

"I don't care why the Fifth Army is here, Harsted, we don't have enough food to—" the man stopped mid-sentence, turning towards Dayne as the doors swung open. "What is the meaning of this? I gave explicit instructions not to be disturbed!"

Dayne flicked his wrist, launching the knife through the air, pushing it forward with threads of Air. The man stumbled backwards as the blade sunk into his throat. He spluttered and choked, his blood spilling out over his hands as he grasped the hilt of the knife.

As Dayne's eyes locked with Harsted Arnim's, pure power surged through his body, chilling his veins, fuelling his rage. He had waited for this for so long. Bided his time. Honed his body. Hunted his prey. This night he would finally have the vengeance he craved. He let go of the Spark, feeling the power ebb from him as he did. He wanted to feel the satisfaction of draining the life from that man's body. Of watching the light fade from his eyes.

Harsted didn't so much as attempt to catch his companion as he fell to the ground. Instead, he ripped two axes from their loops at his hip and turned to face his attacker. The man howled as he charged, swinging one axe through the air while holding the other across his chest.

Without reaching for a weapon, Dayne side-stepped the first swing, and took Harsted's legs out from under him, watching as the man crashed to the ground.

"Get up," Dayne growled, stepping backwards, stopping himself from lunging. He couldn't let this end so quickly.

The man dragged himself to his feet, his face scrunched in a wolf-like snarl, fury burning in his eyes. He moved towards Dayne once more, this time cautiously.

As the next swing came in, Dayne pulled a knife from his belt, deflecting the axe, using the weapon's own momentum to carry it to the left before reversing the swing of his arm and driving the blade into Harsted's shoulder. The man howled, dropping an axe as the blade tore into his flesh.

Dayne pulled the knife free to the sound of ripping skin, blood pouring from the wound. He leapt backwards, out of the reach of a counterstrike. "Do you remember me?"

"I will gut you!" The man lunged forward, swinging his remaining axe at the side of Dayne's head.

Dayne sidestepped, allowing Harsted's axe swing to carry him forward and off balance. As the man careened past, Dayne kicked out, ramming the flat of his foot into the side of the man's knee. A *crunch* sounded, and Harsted collapsed to the floor, screaming in agony.

"I expected more!" Dayne roared, his blood simmering as he stood over the man. Harsted lifted his axe, but Dayne kicked it from the man's grasp, letting it clatter to the stone a few feet away. It didn't matter who heard him now. Nobody could stop Harsted Arnim from dining in Achyron's halls.

"Who are you?" Fury still painted the man's voice as he dragged himself to a semi-seated position, only the slightest traces of fear breaking through the cracks in his facade. Dayne could see the pain in his eyes, blood leaking from the wound in his arm, his hand clasping his shattered knee. Dayne hated himself for admiring how Harsted faced his own death.

"Do you not remember me, Harsted Arnim, Commander of the Fifth Army? It was by your word that thousands of my people burned. By your word that my parents were slaughtered."

The man stared blankly at Dayne, examining him. It took a few moments, but then Dayne saw recognition in Harsted's eyes. "It can't be."

"It is."

"Dayne Ateres…" Harsted spoke as though he himself didn't believe the words that had left his mouth. "I thought you were dead."

"Part of me did die that day. Unfortunately for you, it was the kinder part." Dayne lifted his foot, slamming it down on Harsted's already-shattered knee, feeling bones crunch and snap, splintering beneath the weight of his boot. The scream that left Harsted's throat as he writhed in pain would have once turned Dayne's stomach, but now it did nothing but strengthen his resolve. Dayne lowered himself, resting on his haunches so his eyes were level with Harsted's. "'Burn them all'. That's what you said. Do you remember?"

Harsted pushed himself backwards, gasping as he dragged himself along the floor away from Dayne. "I should have killed you then!"

"You should have," Dayne replied, rising to his full height. "But now, Harsted Arnim, I am the harbinger of your death. I have come to cast judgement over you, just as you did that day."

As Dayne spoke, Harsted continued to drag himself backwards, leaving a trail of blood and shattered bone behind him.

Dayne followed him, keeping his gaze locked on Harsted's as he walked, each step slow and purposeful, a wolf approaching wounded prey. Dayne leaned down, grabbed Harsted by the loops in his armour, and heaved him to his feet, shoving him across the room towards the balcony. He watched as the man stumbled and then collapsed, screaming as his broken knee gave way beneath him. "Harsted Arnim. You are charged with, and have been found guilty of, murder."

As Harsted tried to crawl away, Dayne kicked him in the flat of his back, sending him sprawling to the ground once more. Reaching down, he grabbed the man by the neck of his armour and dragged him across the floor. "You ordered the deaths of thousands of Valtaran citizens. You stood and watched as they were burned alive, their lungs filling with smoke, their skin melting from their bones. You do not hold the right to draw breath."

The brisk night air swept over Dayne's face as he stepped out onto the balcony, dragging Harsted behind him. The body of Lord Gurning lay lifeless on the stone, the knife still lodged in his neck, his blood pooled around him. Reaching the balustrade that framed the balcony, Dayne heaved Harsted to his feet and shoved him against the stone rail. "You must pay the price, and so must those who stood by you. If you give me the name of the Dragonguard, I will spare you unnecessary pain."

"The Dragonguard?" A spluttering laugh escaped Harsted's throat, interrupted only by twitches of pain in his face. "You truly are insane."

"Give me her name."

"Her name is Sylvan Anura." Blood trickled from the corner of Harsted's mouth, his lips forming a forced smile. "I give it to you gladly, for she will peel the skin from your bones."

"We will see." Lifting his hand in one smooth motion, Dayne dragged the knife across Harsted's throat.

As the blood fountained, Harsted clasped his hands around the wound in a futile attempt to stop the flow, his eyes bulging, every breath spluttering.

"As your soul is carried from this world," Dayne said, still holding Harsted in place, blood pouring over his hand. "Make sure you never forget my name again. I am Dayne Ateres. Son of Ilya and Arkin Ateres." With one last look into the man's eyes, Dayne reached for the Spark and pulled on threads of Fire. "What was it you said again? Burn them all?"

Dayne pulled so deeply at the threads that their warmth began to burn his veins, and then he pulled harder. Images of Stormwatch flashed across his mind. The flames. The screams. Rivers of dragonfire pouring from the sky. He could smell the burning flesh in the air. Feel the emptiness in his chest.

Unleashing a visceral scream, he pushed the threads through his hands and engulfed Harsted in a torrent of fire, illuminating the night in a blazing inferno. Even as the flames raged, he pushed harder and harder, fuelling them with every drop of his anger until they burned so hot, he could barely stand it. Then, his energy ebbing, he let go of the threads, took two steps back, and dropped to his knees.

For the past two years Dayne had been consumed by an unrelenting shroud of numbness. It had hardened him, pushed him forward. But as he knelt there, a raging tempest swelling within him, he felt a crack at his core. Tears streamed from his eyes, his shoulders convulsed, and his hands shook. Almost subconsciously, he reached out to the Spark, pulling at threads of Earth and Air, dragging them into himself, feeling their power course through his body. He roared into the night until his lungs burned, slamming his fists against the floor, his hands trembling as cracks spread through the stone.

His chest trembling, his lungs dragging in ragged breaths, Dayne released the threads. He pulled himself to his feet, all the while watching as flames consumed the man who had ripped his life from him. As Harsted's screams faded, the life torn from the man's body, Dayne let the numbness back in, quenching the storm. He wasn't done yet. There was more blood to be spilled.

He walked to the edge of the balcony, climbed onto the balustrade, and jumped, wrapping himself in threads of Air.

Sylvan Anura.

IV

THE HUNTRESS

The smell of piss, damp, and stale beer assaulted Dayne's senses as he heaved open the doors to The Dripping Bucket, letting himself stumble inwards more from momentum than anything else. The common room was packed wall to wall. Traders, soldiers, travellers, beggars, cutpurses, and peasants. The clientele of The Dripping Bucket were as eclectic as any Dayne had ever seen. Everyone was welcome, until they weren't.

Drawing a breath in through his nose, he pushed his way through the drunken crowd, pain pulsing through him with each step. With his body no longer protected by the rush of battle, his muscles had begun to spasm, his bones had started to ache, and the Spark sapped at him, draining his energy like a hole in a keg. He collected a few sideways glances as he pushed his way through, but nothing out of the ordinary. The patrons of the Dripping Bucket were used to seeing people in his state stumble through the inn. In fact, Dayne was near certain that more blood had soaked into the floorboards of the Dripping Bucket than most battlefields.

"You've had a good night then?" the innkeeper asked when Dayne reached the bar. The man was easily a head above Dayne, with a slightly rounded belly, dark hair, and thick beard that sprawled outward from his face like wisps of smoke. He wore a grease-stained white shirt with a leather apron draped over his front that looked as though it had seen more summers than Dayne.

"You could say that," Dayne answered, clenching his jaw as a spasm shot up his back. "Are there any baths free?"

"Aye. I'll have one of the girls fill one with water. Hot or cold?"

"Hot or cold?"

The man shrugged. "Hot costs coin, cold costs less coin."

Dayne sighed before reaching into his pocket and pulling out a small cloth pouch. He pulled open the drawstrings and slid a silver coin across the counter to the innkeeper.

"Cold it is."

Dayne narrowed his eyes and glared at the man. Reluctantly, he produced another silver coin and tossed it down beside the first. "You're a fucking thief, not an innkeeper."

"And you're not a soldier," the man said with a toothy grin, nodding towards the red and black leather armour that covered Dayne's body.

Reaching into his pouch, Dayne produced two more silver coins and placed them on the counter.

The innkeeper laughed, snatched up the coins and yelled back into the kitchen. "One of you wenches fill a bath for Master Hunter here. Hot."

His call was answered by a screeching shout followed by the sound of pots and pans clanging.

"Your bath will be ready in a few minutes. The door at the end of the hallway behind the stairs." With that, the man turned and began yelling at two patrons who were beating lumps out of each other at the other end of the bar.

His muscles urging him to move quicker, Dayne pushed through the crowd once more, making his way up the staircase on the left side of the common room. Once he reached his room, he pushed the door open, kicked off his boots, and dropped himself onto the edge of the rickety old bed.

The room was closer to a cell than anything else, no longer than eight feet, no wider than five. There were no windows, and the bed, with its rusted frame and worryingly damp mattress, took up all but the slightest bit of floor-space. The only source of light was a fragile-looking candle sitting in a holder atop a rotting wooden shelf beside the door.

Reaching down, Dayne stuck his hand underneath the bed and pulled out his worn leather satchel – the same one he had taken with him from Skyfell.

After few moments of searching, Dayne produced a small notebook, a pen, and an inkwell. With particular care, he undid the strip of leather that held the book closed. A length of orange silk ribbon bound to the inside of the book kept track of the last page Dayne had opened. Following the ribbon, Dayne opened the book and stared at the page for a moment. It held two names:

Loren Koraklon
Harsted Arnim

He placed the inkwell on his lap, unscrewed the lid, and dipped the pen into the ink. Then, letting out a breath, he crossed Harsted Arnim's name off the list. A sense of relief washed through him, followed by a pang of guilt which he quickly pushed down – a skill he had become quite adept at over the past two years.

"He deserved it," he whispered, screwing the lid of the inkwell back on. Images flashed through Dayne's mind. Images of blood fountaining from the man's throat, of the flames consuming him. *He deserved every damn second of it.*

Dayne stared at the page for a few more moments before adding a third name to the list. A name he had been searching for: Sylvan Anura. There were others on the ship that day, but those three needed to die.

Tilting his head back, he let out a long sigh before replacing the lid of the inkwell, closing the notebook, and laying everything on the bed beside him. Reaching further into the satchel, he produced a white linen towel and a bar of junil oil soap, scented with lavender and wrapped in cheese cloth.

His gaze lingered on the soap. Blood could be washed from a man's skin, but it would always stain his soul. Dayne had ended one hundred and forty-three lives in the pursuit of Harsted Arnim. Each one bringing him a small step closer to his goal. There was nothing that could cleanse those marks. *I do what must be done.*

The drunken revelry in the common room was still in full swing as Dayne left his room, pushed his way down the stairs, through the crowd, and back towards the hallway that led to the bathing room.

The dark, dingy hallway stretched on for just over fifty feet, black mould spreading across its roof like moss on a forest floor. Twelve doors were set into the wall at either side, each one built from a wood that had seen its best days in the years before Dayne was born. The more Dayne thought about it, it seemed that he must have had one of the more *luxurious* rooms in the inn. Twelve rooms on each side, stretched over a fifty-foot hallway meant each room was only just wider than four feet. *More coffin than room.*

Reaching the end of the corridor, he threw the linen towel over his shoulder, turned the door handle, and stepped through.

The bathing room was about half the size of the common room, with six oblong wooden baths that stood about five feet apart, each stained a dark brown and banded with iron. In truth, they looked a far sight better than what Dayne had expected. The fact that they weren't leaking and didn't smell of piss were both positives in his opinion.

The only other person in the room was a dark-skinned woman, Narvonan by the look of her, who sat in the bath at the far right, her arms strewn over the edges of the wood, her head resting on the rim behind her, eyes closed.

Turning his attention from the woman, Dayne moved towards the bath closest to him, which was filled about two thirds, steam rising from the surface of the water. The closer he stepped to the bath the more his muscles ached and groaned, as though anticipating the relief the hot water would provide.

Dayne set the towel and soap down on a small side table that stood not a foot off the ground to the side of the bath. Grunting, he undid the straps on the blood-stained Lorian leathers and tossed them in a heap beside the bath. He then peeled off his shirt, the dried blood cracking as it was pulled away from his skin. He folded the shirt and set it beside the towel; it was followed by his shoes, socks, and trousers – in that order, leaving his shoes side by side at the foot of the table. Even damaged, covered in dirt, and crusted with blood, he still couldn't fight the compulsion to fold and arrange his clothes. *"Regiment and discipline,"* his father had said. *"The makings of a soldier, and the necessities of a man."*

An involuntary sigh escaped him as his right foot broke the surface of the water, the heat coming close to scalding him. After a few seconds of letting his body adjust, he lifted his left foot in, then carefully lowered himself into the hot bath, feeling his body ache as he did. He watched as the dirt and blood lifted from his skin, spreading out in circles, tainting the colour of the water to a murky reddish-black.

Dayne picked up the soap, removed the cheesecloth, and proceeded to scrub his body until his skin begged for mercy. Reaching back, he dug his fingers into the muscles at the back of his neck, pressing down, groaning as he tilted his head to the side. He sat there for a while, soaking in the bloody water, his eyes half glazed over as his mind wandered. Alina would be nearing her fourteenth summer now, Baren his nineteenth. He had failed them both. He had left them to be tied to Lorian strings, puppets. "There was nothing I could do," he whispered, burying his hands into the corners of his eyes. "I…"

Dayne let his sentence trail off at the sound of breaking water. Lifting his head from his hands, he opened his eyes and looked towards the source of the sound: the other occupied tub. For a moment, everything seemed normal. The dark-skinned woman just lay there, her head tilted back, her eyes closed, a broad smile on her face. But then, just as he was about to return to his thoughts, another head emerged from beneath the water's surface. A blonde-haired woman. She giggled as she lifted herself up and planted a kiss on the other woman's lips.

Dayne shook his head and laughed quietly to himself, embracing the momentary relief from the melancholy that followed him. He knew the woman had looked far too happy for someone bathing in a place like this. Dayne felt the heat of his cheeks reddening as his eyes locked with dark-skinned woman's, who was now staring directly at him. She gave him a wink, turning her attention back towards the other woman, running her fingers through the tangle of blonde hair.

Without a word, Dayne leaned back into the bath, closing his eyes, the moment of laughter leaving him. What he would have given to have Mera there with him. To feel her touch, her warmth. Even as children, her light had always pulled him from the darkness. *I will return to you. I promise. I will kill Sylvan Anura, and then I will drive a blade through Loren Koraklon's heart.*

After a while, he heard the two women exit the bath. The breaking of water, the dripping on stone, the giggling. He waited until the sounds had dissipated and was about to open his eyes and sit up when a woman's voice. "You don't mind company, do you?"

Dayne jerked up, snapping his eyes open, instinctively reaching for the Spark. He could feel its power pulsating in the back of his mind. The elemental strands coiling around each other, each one distinct, and yet not.

His eyes locked with the woman's, his heart thumping as he refrained from pulling at the threads of Air that waited for him. The woman stood beside the bath, naked as the day she was born.

"I'm perfectly fine on my own," Dayne answered, shifting in the bath, reaching for the bar of soap, watching the woman's hands for any sudden movement.

As though he hadn't spoken, she lifted a leg and stepped into the bath. "It's just," she said, lifting her other foot in and setting herself down into the water opposite Dayne. "I couldn't help but notice you staring."

The woman had eyes so dark they were almost black. Her stare sent a chill down his spine. She wasn't looking at him, she was looking inside him. Even still, he held eye contact. He would not let her win. "I wasn't staring."

"You were staring."

"I wasn't."

"You were." The woman's tone turned flat, as though the conversation was over and she had been victorious.

Dayne held the woman's gaze, trying his best to seem unperturbed by the whole situation. Though he was pretty certain he wasn't succeeding.

"Don't worry," the woman said, a wry smile curling her lips. "You're not my type." She gave Dayne a wink almost identical to the one she had given him before.

"Well, then why are you here?" Dayne shifted back a bit in the bath, trying to create more space between himself and the woman.

"I'm here for a *very* different reason." Every muscle in Dayne's body tensed as the feeling of cold steel touched the side of his neck. "Now, now, now. Relax. Don't try anything stupid because that would end badly. For you, not for me. I'd be fine. If I wanted you dead, I wouldn't have spoken. I simply would have slit your throat from ear to ear. You never would have heard a thing."

Without moving his neck, Dayne looked down and to his left to see the woman's leg was now out of the water, her foot beside his neck, water dripping, toes wrapped around a long needle, about an inch thick, with a point that looked as though it could pierce steel. *She moves like a viper.*

"What do you want?" Dayne said, his eyes not leaving hers, still holding on to the Spark. "I have nothing of value."

"Oh, but that's where you're wrong, *Dayne Ateres*. Somebody has put quite a large amount of gold on your head. And I like gold."

"How do you know my name?" Dayne's pulse quickened, his blood thumping through his veins.

To his surprise, the woman actually laughed, a look of incredulity spreading across her face. "That was probably the stupidest question I have ever heard. You, quite literally, have the sigil of House Ateres tattooed on your chest. I'm sure that seemed like a good idea at the time, but it's not ideal for hiding who you are."

"Who wants me dead?"

The woman didn't answer, instead, she continued staring at him, her eyebrow raised as though he had just asked the second stupidest question she had ever heard. Her leg was still protruding from the water, the tip of the needle pressed against his neck.

"All right. What do you want?"

"I either want my body's weight in gold or a very damn good reason not to kill you."

"I don't have any gold."

The woman shrugged. "Well then, you better have a damn good reason for me not to kill you."

"I don't have one."

"Don't lie to me, Dayne Ateres. I've seen the look in your eyes. I know when someone has blood yet to spill."

"If you're going to kill me, then kill me." Dayne pressed his neck into the needle, his stare unwavering, the threads of Air still waiting for his mind's touch.

"I didn't say I was going to kill you. I said if you didn't give me my bodyweight in gold or give me a damn good reason not to kill you, *then* I would kill you. The little details matter," she said with a shrug. "Did your father never teach you that?"

"My father is dead."

The woman grimaced, raising a fist to her chin. "Actually, I knew that. Apologies. Sentiment remains though. The little things *do* matter."

Dayne narrowed his eyes, tilting his head sideways. He couldn't decide if the woman was a genius, or if she had lost her mind.

"All right," the woman said, turning her bottom lip. "Meet me in the common room once you're dry. There's something about having you staring at my tits that just doesn't make this seem as serious."

"I'm not staring!" Dayne lifted his arms in defence.

"Why are you not staring? They're fabulous." The woman glared at Dayne as though offended.

"What? Why… I didn't mean to…"

"Oh, relax. They're just tits. Why do men always get so worked up about tits?" Out of the corner of his eye, Dayne saw the needle pull away from his neck, sinking back into the water, along with the woman's leg as she pulled herself from the tub, water rolling down her naked skin. She walked over towards the other tub, all the while still holding the long needle in her toes, dried herself lightly, then grabbed a long dress the colour of the setting sun and threw it on.

"I'll wait for you in the common room."

"What if I don't show?"

"I'll hunt you down and kill you in your sleep, and you'll never see tits again."

Dayne hoisted himself up so he was sitting upright in the bath. "I wasn't… fuck it. Who in the name of the gods are you?"

"My name's Belina," the woman said, tossing her towel over her shoulder, "Belina Louna."

Dayne stood at the door into the common room for what felt like hours before taking a deep breath, pushing it open, and stepping through.

He had thought about running. There was a door at the corner of the bathing room that led to the kitchens and then out to the street. He could have been ten miles away on horseback before she even realised he was gone. But if this woman had found him here, he had no doubt she would be able to find him again. Better to face her head-on.

It only took him a few seconds to find her, sitting in the corner of the inn, her sunset-orange dress a beacon amidst the mottled browns, green, and blacks of the inn. Where others fell about themselves, pouring ale down their throats and singing at the top of their lungs, Belina sat quietly, waiting, staring out the dirt-covered window at the night sky beyond. Her black hair was tied into tight braids that fell down past her shoulders, and the light from the tallow candle on the table cast a soft glow against her dark skin. Had Dayne not known any better, he would have though her almost peaceful.

Dayne had barely another moment to reconsider his decision before she turned her head and her eyes met his. She raised one eyebrow, gesturing to the seat across from her.

He crossed the inn, weaving in and out of the crowd as he did. By instinct, his hand fell to his hip. No knives, no weapons of any kind. If he left this table alive, he would never be so foolish again. His eyes flashed to the entrance of the inn – a set of double doors, no more than twenty feet from the table. A second route was through the kitchen behind the bar. A third through the door behind him. But the easiest would be the window beside the table. The wood was mouldy, crumbling – weak. If he tucked his hands beneath his armpits, he would avoid the worst of the breaking glass.

The window it is.

"You came," Belina said, puffing her bottom lip out.

Dayne sat himself on the chair across from her, his gaze never leaving hers as he rested his arms on the table. "You didn't think I would?"

"I hoped you would."

Silence gripped the air as both Dayne and Belina studied each other. He could see the look in her eyes. Could feel her weighing him, measuring him.

"What do you want, Dayne?" Belina asked, breaking the silence, leaning forward, resting her elbows on the edge of the table, her hands clasped together.

"You're the one who wants something," Dayne answered, keeping his tone level, his gaze locked.

The hardness of Belina's stare set Dayne's pulse racing. "What do *you* want?"

Dayne swallowed, his mouth growing dry. He became suddenly aware of his fingers tapping against the damp wood of the table, moving of their own volition. He forced them to stop. Two years he had walked the land. Two years. By blade and by blood, he had carved a path through Epheria in search of Harsted Arnim. In search of the one name he had learned that night. In search of answers. In search of vengeance. That path had led him from Skyfell to Oberwall. From Berona to Catagan. And finally, to where he sat right now. In all that time, he hadn't once said the words out loud. "I want to slaughter those who took my parents from me. I want to run my blade through Sylvan Anura's heart, so she may taste death and so I may return to Valtara, where I will strip the flesh from Loren Koraklon's bones. But more than anything, I want to feel the warm embrace of my brother and my sister. I want to let them know that I never stopped thinking of them. I want to let them know that I will *always* protect them."

The silence that followed Dayne's words was deafening. It reduced all sounds around them to a low drone that thrummed in the back of his mind. Voices faded, clattering tankards turned to dull thumps, stamping feet became nothing but a vibration through the floorboards. It was as though the words had shifted a weight within him, granted some form of relief to the burden he carried.

Slowly, Belina leaned back in her chair, lifting her arms from the table and crossing them. "You had me right up until the whole 'embracing your brother and sister part'," she said with a shrug. "I'm not really a touchy-feely kind of person. Unless it's the right kind of touchy-feely, but that's a whole different conversation." Sitting forward, Belina looked into Dayne's eyes. This close, he could see the gold-speckled brown of her irises. "I cannot promise you revenge. That is yours to take. But I know that name – Sylvan Anura. She is one of the Dragonguard. You wouldn't get within five feet of her with blood still in your veins. It may take years, but if you come with me, I will teach you ways to take a life that you had never thought possible. I will help you put that blade to her throat. What's more, I will bring you to a man who can find her. A man well versed in killing her kind."

"What do you want in return? What is your stake in my vengeance?"

"I want *you*, Dayne Ateres. I want your blade. I have a list of lives that require ending. A list that tethers me in place, binds me to this life. If you help me cut that tether, you will have your vengeance, or we will both die in the trying."

"Who are they?" Dayne asked, turning his gaze to his open palms. So much blood painted them already. "These people we are to kill."

"Servants of the empire – mostly. The same people who put a price on your head."

Dayne nodded absently, staring at the table, staring at nothing. "And you know someone who can bring me to Sylvan Anura?"

"I do. He used to be one of them, before The Fall – a Draleid. Now, he is their hunter."

"How do I know you are telling the truth? How can I trust you?"

"Because I let you live. I could have killed you months ago when I found you in Berona. Or again, when you slept in the trees of Kingswood, or under the stars by the Trorq River. But I didn't."

"You've been following me all this time?"

Belina nodded, her expression unchanging.

Dayne bit down on his top lip, scratching at the stubble on his chin. After a few long moments, he lifted his gaze, meeting Belina's stare. "We have a deal."

PART 3

TEMPERED IN BLOOD

FIVE YEARS LATER

V

OLD ROPES

Fifteen miles south of Elkenrim, Loria
Year 3075 after doom

Sheets of rain hammered down from charcoal skies as Dayne stood beneath the edge of the forest canopy, his hand extended, droplets breaking against his palm. Before him, the ground rolled downwards towards an old dirt road, now mostly muddied, and then back up into the woodland on the other side.

The night air whipped around him, nipping at his skin, causing his cloak to ripple and billow. Even beneath the protection of the canopy, his clothes were near soaked through, and droplets fell from his nose and chin.

They had arrived almost two hours ago, so as to set themselves and to allow their eyes to adjust to the darkness. Even in the dim light of the waning moon, he could see the ripples of raindrops in the puddles on the road. "Are you ready?"

Belina stepped up beside him, a black mantle draped over her shoulders. She stared at the road for a few moments before turning to face him, dark hair matted to her skin by rainfall. "Five years and you still ask stupid questions."

Dayne couldn't help but laugh, the white of Belina's teeth betraying her smile. "Five years and you still don't give straight answers."

"And I never will." Belina winked, turning to look back out over the road below. All mirth left her voice as she stared off into the blackness. "This is the last one, Dayne. We do this, and I am free. Then we take you to Sylvan Anura." Belina looked back at him, her eyes glinting in the moonlight. "Don't fuck it up."

Dayne let the slightest of smiles touch his lips. There was no happiness in it; it was more a reflex than anything else. "I'll try not to."

It was at least another half hour, by Dane's reckoning, before the slopping, sucking sounds of horse hooves in mud travelled through the valley, carrying on the night air. A few moments later, the dim orange glow of lanterns broke through the blanket of night.

"Sixteen riders and a two-horse carriage, large enough for four. They're already struggling with the mud," Dayne whispered, threads of Fire and Spirit enhancing his vision aided by the light from the lanterns that hung from the carriage.

"Good. Remember, this needs to look like bandits. Do what we planned, and no more of that hand wavy shit than is needed."

"I don't wave my hands."

"I've seen you do it.

"Fuck off, Belina."

Dayne could only see the back of Belina's hood, but he didn't have to see her face to know she was grinning from ear to ear.

Shaking his head, Dayne reached back and pulled his leather bow sleeve from around his shoulders, opened the straps, and removed his bow and string. He tossed the sleeve back into place and set about stringing the bow. He ran his finger along the string, plucking at it, more from habit than anything else.

"Wait for it…" Belina whispered, her voice only just rising over the drumming of the rain on Dayne's hood.

"Belina, I know—"

"Waaait for it…"

"I fucking hate you," Dayne whispered, shaking his head. He closed his eyes, the world turning black, his mind illuminated by the elemental strands pulsating with energy, twisting and snaking around each other. Still pulling on threads of Fire and Spirit, he reached out and plucked at threads of Earth and Water, pulling them into his body, feeling the cool touch of the Water wash over his skin and the rough grate of Earth as it filled his bones.

"Wait…"

The drum of hooves grew louder, battering against the sodden earth. With his mind open to the Spark, everything felt clearer, sharper.

"…now!"

Opening his eyes, Dayne pulled harder on the threads of Earth and Water, driving them forward, funnelling them into the ground below, softening the earth even further, saturating it to a point that it became nothing short of quicksand.

The cries of the horses echoed through the valley as their hooves sunk into the liquid earth, their momentum sending them tumbling, legs breaking, blood spraying. Pure chaos.

Dayne didn't have to look to know Belina was already halfway down the hill, her knives drawn, her line set for the carriage. He cast his eyes over the scene, assessing. Five riders had fallen, two crushed beneath their horses, three scrambling to regain their footing. Two riders were stuck in the mud but had managed to stay on horseback. The other nine were circling around the carriage. He pulled an arrow from the quiver on his back, nocking it, drawing in a breath as he drew the string. Loose. The rider closest to the carriage fell, the arrow taking him in the side of the head.

Dayne drew again, raindrops snaking down his forehead, dripping from his eyebrows. Loose. Another rider fell from his horse, an arrow slicing through the side of his neck, blood pluming out the other side.

Six more times he drew, and six more times blood spilled into the mud, pooling in murky water. By the time Belina reached the carriage, only six of the guards remained; two were still on horseback, four now on their feet.

Taking his bow in one hand, Dayne started down the hill towards the road. The rain had turned the ground beneath his feet to sludge, and it was all he could do to stay on his feet. Belina had made it look so easy, as she always did.

Halfway down, a glint of steel flashed in the night to Belina's left. Dayne stuck out his left foot and pushed himself back, letting his backside slam into the mud. As he did, he slipped an arrow from his quiver, nocking and loosing it as quick as his hands could move. A brief whistle ripped through the air and then stopped, the arrow punching into the man's chest.

Heaving himself to his feet, Dayne continued down the hill, his legs and torso burning as his muscles struggled to keep him upright. Five guards left, two on horseback, three on foot.

Belina moved in a flash of steel. Four guards left. One on horseback, three on their feet.

As Dayne reached the bottom of the hill and stepped out onto the road, he pushed threads of Earth and Water into the soil, solidifying the ground in front of him as he moved. He lengthened his strides, sprinting towards the carriage. Belina had disappeared around the other side, but the sounds of steel on steel let him know that she had found at least one of the guards.

A shout rose to Dayne's left as a guard charged towards him, the hood of the man's black cloak blowing off his face as he hefted his sword.

Shifting his feet, Dayne moved to meet the man's charge. He gripped his bow in one hand, then tossed it in the air towards the guard, who raised his arm to protect himself. As the bow clattered off the man's forearm, Dayne slipped a knife from the strap across his chest and launched it into the man's throat, blood spraying black in the dark.

Feet slapping against the mud sounded to Dayne's right. He reached up, snatching his bow out of the air before dropping to one knee, twisting towards the sound. His fingers brushed against the goose feather fletching as he pulled an arrow from his quiver. Two beats of his heart. He loosed, close enough to hear the *thunk* as the arrow sank into the charging guard's neck. Blood poured out over the shaft, the guard dropping to their knees in the mud.

Slowly, dragging air in through his nostrils, Dayne rose to his feet. He walked over to the guard and placed his hand around the shaft of the arrow. "May The Mother embrace you," he said as he planted his foot on the guard's chest and kicked forward, pulling the arrow free.

The guard fell into the mud with a slap, gasping as blood spurted from the now open wound in his neck.

Wiping the arrow on his trouser leg, Dayne slipped it back into his quiver, slung the bow over his shoulder, and drew his knife. Except for the pummelling of rain, the night was silent.

When he reached the other side of the carriage, Dayne found Belina standing in the rain, her hood drawn, her cloak and hair saturated, a knife in each hand, and two bodies lying motionless at her feet.

"That's all of them," he said, looking over the two bodies.

Belina didn't answer. Her gaze was fixed on the carriage door, her chest rising and falling in slow, measured breaths, the rain falling around her, streaks of water rolling down her face. She gave a nod, then approached the carriage.

Reaching forward, she pulled down the handle and swung the door open, blocking Dayne's view.

"I knew you would come for me." The voice was followed by a hooded figure who stepped from the carriage, his feet sinking into the mud. The man walked past Belina, as though she didn't have murder in her eyes. He took three steps then turned. "When I heard of the others, I knew it was you."

Dayne tilted his head, trying to get a look at the man beneath the hood, but shadows obscured his face.

"If you wanted out, you should have just asked, Belina."

Belina took a step towards the man. Dayne recognised the look that flashed across her face: pure hatred. It was the same thing that festered within him whenever he thought of Sylvan Anura. "You and I both know you never would have allowed that. You would have had me killed. This was the only way. Now kneel."

"Yes," the man said, his voice almost a whisper, his fingers clasped together in a thoughtful pose. "You are probably correct."

"Kneel."

"Surely, you will allow an old man to die on his feet?"

"I said *kneel*!" Belina kicked the side of the man's knee, eliciting a gasp as he fell, mud splattering as he crashed into the churned earth, catching himself with his hands.

Dayne reached his hand out, his voice soft, "Belina—"

The look in Belina's eyes cut Dayne short: sorrow, fury, loss.

"Do you regret *anything*?" Belina asked, her words pushing through gritted teeth as she stood over the man. Dayne could see the knife shaking in her hand. In five years, he had never seen her like this. Belina never faltered. *Who is he?*

"I have many regrets, contrary to what you might believe." The man lifted his head to meet Belina's gaze. "Many things I wish I could change. Many paths I wish I had trodden."

Reaching down, Belina pulled back the man's hood, revealing the face of a man who had seen at least sixty summers, his skin dark and furrowed by time, his hair white as bone.

"To which god do you pledge your soul?" Belina asked, wrapping her fingers through the man's hair, pulling his head back, staring into his eyes.

Silence followed, the drumming of rain the only sound.

A resigned sigh escaped the man. "I pledge my soul to Elyara, The Maiden, wisest of all, in hopes that she may guide my mind."

Belina nodded. She looked as though she were going to say something, but her lips remained shut. Dayne had never known a sharper mind than hers. Always so full of wit. It unsettled him to see her so silent. "I pray she accepts your pledge."

With that, the man closed his eyes and tilted his head back even further, exposing his throat. "It is good that it is you."

No sooner had the words left his lips than Belina drew the blade across his throat, parting skin and drawing blood. The man fell backwards into the mud, blood spraying from his neck, his body jerking as it attempted to cling to life.

Belina stood still as he died, rain soaking her, dripping from her nose and the ends of her hair. Dayne had seen her take countless lives in the years they had travelled together. She never took pleasure in it, but neither had it ever seemed to unnerve her. This was different.

"It is done," she said, kneeling beside the body, running her hand along the man's cheek. "Thank you, Dayne. This wouldn't have been possible without you." She rose to her feet, the knife still shaking in her hand. As she turned to Dayne, he could have sworn he saw tears running down her cheeks, but it was near impossible to tell with the rainfall. "Now it is time I honour my end of our agreement. We ride for Gildor in the morning."

Belina made to walk past Dayne, back up the hill to where they had tied their horses, but Dayne placed a hand on her shoulder, halting her. "Who was that, Belina?"

When Belina lifted her gaze to meet his, Dayne was sure tears filled her eyes. "My father."

VI

YOU CAN REST NOW

Seventy miles south of Gildor, Loria

The wind buffeted the mountainside, sweeping sheets of snow this way and that, forcing the trees to bend and creak, their needle thin leaves spraying white dust into the air. Dayne pulled his coat tighter around himself, trudging through the blanket of snow that covered the ground, his feet sinking in an inch or so with each step. Thick pine forests spread out either side, stretching off into the distance, swallowed by the snowfall. Ahead, the jagged peaks of Mar Dorul reached towards the sky, dark and ominous, looming over the landscape like an eldritch god. Against Mar Dorul, the Rolling Mountains of Valtara seemed like gentle hills.

"Where are we meeting him?" Dayne asked, turning to Belina, who slogged along beside him, a heavy, fur-lined winter coat draped over her shoulders, her hood flapping in the wind. Dayne tried his best to keep his teeth from chattering, but it was a futile effort. He had seen snow cap the peaks of the Rolling Mountains in the winter months, but he had never before seen it so close, never felt its frigid embrace.

Belina reached out a hand, extending a gloved finger. "We will wait for him there," she said, pointing towards a large, oblong stone that jutted from the ground a few hundred feet away.

Dayne nodded, dropped his head, and kept walking, fighting against the wind as it attempted to throw him back down the mountainside.

By the time they reached the standing stone, Dayne's chest burned from the icy air, and his legs groaned in complaint. He reached up, brushing a coat of snow from the side of the stone, his fingers falling into grooves that had been carved into its surface. "It's been over a month getting here and you still haven't said anything about Elkenrim."

"There's nothing to say." Belina stared off into the snowfall as she spoke, her hands tucked into her coat pockets, her tone flat.

"Damn it, Belina. You could have told me."

"Told you what?" Belina's voice rose as she turned, her eyes cold.

"That we were hunting your father!"

"What difference would it have made? My father put a blade in my fist before I'd seen my fifth summer. He committed me to the Hand just after I'd seen my twelfth. He was cold, ruthless, and I was nothing but a tool to him. I bore no love for the man who called himself my father."

Dayne held Belina's gaze, a knot twisting in his chest. As high as Belina's walls were, they now held visible cracks.

"Don't look at me like that." Belina took a step towards Dayne. "I don't need your pity."

"You should have told me," Dayne repeated, softer.

For a moment, he thought Belina might roar at him, or strike out, but then her gaze gentled and she reached out her arm. "I will from now on."

"By blade and by blood," Dayne said, clasping his hand around Belina's forearm, allowing a smile to touch the edge of his lips.

"By blade and by blood," Belina replied, before twisting her lips into a pout. "I need to hear more of these Valtaran sayings. I think I would fit right in there."

"That you would. Though you'd probably have your tongue cut out pretty quickly."

"They can fucking try!"

Dayne let go of Belina's arm, struggling to fight back the laughter, when a voice sounded behind them.

"Belina Louna. Thank you for coming."

As he turned, Dayne's hand dropped to the pommel of his sword, more by instinct than anything else.

The man who stood before them was garbed in a greenish-brown hooded cloak that billowed out behind him. The drawstrings of his hood were tied tight, with only a few strands of silvery hair escaping.

"I'm not here out of the goodness of my heart," Belina replied, walking towards the stranger without hesitation and pulling him into a tight embrace. Dayne had never seen her embrace anyone so warmly. In fact, he'd never seen her embrace anyone whatsoever. In her own words, she wasn't exactly the 'touchy-feely type'. "It's good to see you. You look even younger than the last time I saw you.

Have you been eating children again? No? I see your sense of humour is still exactly the same. Dayne Ateres"—Belina turned towards Dayne, holding out her arm—"Meet Therin Eiltris. Elf. Wanderer. Humourless."

Therin stepped forward, throwing a sideways glance at Belina as he lowered his hood to reveal a head of long, silver hair, a sharp face that looked as though it had seen no more than thirty summers, and ears that tapered to a point at the ends. Dayne had met a few elves on his travels, but he had never spent much time with them. Most of what he knew of their kind were simply stories. Old tales twisted and altered by the whispers of time. He nodded his head ever so slightly. "It's a pleasure."

"The pleasure is all mine, Dayne." Therin gave a smile as he spoke. "I knew your mother. She was a kind soul."

With just those words, Dayne felt his heart tear. A gaping hole opened in his chest, stealing the air from his lungs. It genuinely surprised him how quickly he felt tears form at the corners of his eyes. He wanted to speak, but words abandoned him.

"So," Belina said, her gaze softening as she stepped past Dayne, turning to face both of her companions. "Therin, you told me you would bring us to Aeson if we helped you with an issue here. What's that issue?"

"Yes, I—"

"Aeson Virandr?" There was nothing Dayne could do to keep the surprise from his voice, his words escaping his throat before he could stop them.

"One and the same," Belina replied, raising a curious eyebrow. "You know him?"

"I do. What does Aeson Virandr have to do with any of this?"

Belina's eyes narrowed as she stepped towards Dayne. "He is the one who can bring us to Sylvan Anura."

Out of the corner of his eye, Dayne saw Therin's expression shift at the sound of Sylvan's name.

"If we help Therin here, then he will bring us to Aeson, who will bring us to Sylvan. Is there a problem?"

Dayne tapped each of his fingers against his thumbs, moving from his index to his pinkie and then back again. Aeson Virandr was not the name he had expected to hear. He was not sure how he felt about the man. It was Aeson who had helped his mother and father organise the rebellion. He who had stoked the fires and moved the pieces. But where had he been when they needed him?

"No," Dayne said finally, forcing his fingers to stop fidgeting. "No problem."

Belina leaned in closer, her eyes narrowing even further. For a moment, Dayne thought she was going to challenge him, but she didn't. "Good. Therin, lead the way."

"There is an outpost about four hours hike north of here," Therin said, marching through the snow. "I have reason to believe that many of my people are being held within. Children among them. It used to be an old imperial outpost, but it was abandoned years ago. Not three weeks gone, someone escaped, and one of my contacts found them curled up in a family barn not three miles from here. Their wounds were…" The elf's voice trailed off before he regained his composure. "They didn't survive long, but they were able to tell us where they were being held."

"Do you have any idea who controls the outpost now?" Belina asked, her hands tucked in her coat pockets as she walked, small snowflakes melting at her cheek's touch.

"I believe it is still under imperial control, though not officially. I'm not sure what they're doing to my people in there, but I can't let it continue."

"You must be very desperate if I'm the first person you thought of," Belina said, letting out a deep laugh. "What was it you called me the last time we met? 'Blood Merchant'? It's no wonder you're a storyteller – that's the most creative name for an assassin I've heard in a long time." Belina shrugged, her hands still lodged firmly in her pockets. "I've actually used it quite a few times, myself. You should see the look on people's faces when I tell them I'm a *Blood Merchant.*"

To Dayne's surprise, Therin laughed, shaking his head at Belina. "You truly haven't changed in the slightest, have you? But no, you weren't the first person I thought of, surprisingly. You're just the only one who is currently available and willing."

"That hurts, but I'll take it," Belina said with a shrug. A shrug tended to be Belina's most common reaction to just about everything. There never seemed to be a situation that didn't call for a shrug.

Therin and Belina continued chatting as they made their way up the snow-covered mountainside. Dayne kept his mouth shut, listening. He had never seen someone hold their own against Belina's wit, but the elf did that and then some. And by the way he carried himself, Dayne was sure Therin was no stranger to a blade either.

The further they walked, the steeper and narrower the path became, sheer walls of snow-dusted rock rising either side, blocking out most of the sun's light. Dayne had heard stories of Mar Dorul when he was little, or rather nightmares told aloud. A vast landscape of jagged mountains that stretched for hundreds of miles in all directions, its peaks threatening to tear the sky asunder, so tainted by Efialtír's touch that not a single tree or plant grew within its bounds. Even as Dayne slogged through the snow, he could feel a tangible weight hanging in the air, thick as fog. They would find nothing good in this place, of that, he was certain.

After nearly four hours of hiking ever upward through the snow-covered mountain, the rock face on the left fell away, and the path snaked around the side of the mountain, revealing a sheer drop that seemed to have no bottom. Even in the thinning snowfall, Dayne could see nothing but mountains and wide sweeping valleys of emptiness all around him.

He rolled his neck, eliciting a series of cracks born of stiffness. His heavy coat held little protection against the probing cold that bit at any sliver of exposed skin. Once this was done, he would be more than happy if he were to never see snow again as long as he lived. But for now, there was nothing he could do other than tuck his chin in tight and keep walking. Left foot, right foot.

He hadn't noticed Therin had stopped until he just about walked into the elf. "What's wrong?" Dayne asked, stepping up beside Therin, his head tilted down to avoid the chilling wind.

"We're here."

Begrudgingly, Dayne lifted his head, eyes widening. An enormous chasm split the mountains in half, dropping endlessly downward. Set on the same side of the chasm as

Dayne, Belina, and Therin was a stone bastion broken into three storeys, each storey ringed by battlements. The structure rose over a hundred feet into the air, backing onto the mountain on one side and the sheer cliff edge on the other. An enormous stone bridge jutted from the third storey of the bastion, spanning the width of the chasm, connecting to a keep that looked as though it had been built straight into the mountain on the other side, its walls tunnelling into the rockface as though hewn from the mountain itself, smooth and grey, rising almost twice the height of the bastion.

"I thought you said it was an outpost," Belina called to Therin. "That's a fucking fortress!"

"Look," Therin replied, pointing towards the bastion. "The battlements are empty, and I can't see so much as a flicker of light from within. By my guess, they're keeping a skeleton garrison to avoid attracting Uraks."

"It's a little bigger than I expected," Dayne said, casting his gaze over the empty battlements of the bastion, along the enormous stone bridge, then onwards to the keep on the other side of the chasm. He drew his face into a glare at the sound of Belina giggling beside him. "Belina, grow up."

"What? It's better to be bigger than expected. Right, Therin? Better that than the other way around."

The elf gave Belina a flat stare but otherwise didn't answer.

"I swear, one of these days I'm going to die a gruesome death, and when I'm gone, you'll miss my fabulous sense of humour. So, what's the plan?"

"We go in." Without waiting for a response, Therin set off towards the bastion, his snow-dusted coat flapping behind him.

"Elves," Belina said. "Such a penchant for the dramatic. Come on. Hopefully the place is empty." Belina shrugged, then set off after Therin.

Dayne shivered as he approached the stone structure, but it was not born of the cold. The silence that filled the air was eerie. On the side of a mountain like this, even the smallest of sounds should carry, yet he heard nothing but the crunch of snow underfoot. The place seemed completely devoid of life.

Iron braced double doors were set into the front wall of the bastion, standing over fifteen feet high and twice that again in width.

"Barred from the inside." Therin held the palm of his hand against the door as he spoke.

A tingle ran down Dayne's neck, the same one he always felt when someone near him was drawing from the Spark. Groans of stiff iron rose on the other side of the doors, followed by a series of clicks and the sound of metal hitting stone.

Therin leaned forward, eliciting an echoing creak from the enormous door as it swung inwards, its hinges stiff and aged.

While the outside of the bastion had given Dayne an eerie feeling, the inside set every hair on end. The giant door opened to a long, arched corridor that led to a central chamber. Every inch of stone was dusted with snow and laced with cobwebs. The wind whistled as it rushed through the open doorway, sweeping spirals of icy white into the air, carrying them on down the corridor. Here and there, evidence of past occupation littered the ground: a long table crusted with frost, a rusted shield, a copper pot that now held a greenish hue. Nothing pointed to the structure being garrisoned in the previous decade, and yet, Dayne couldn't shake the feeling that he was being watched. "I don't like it. It's too quiet. Too empty."

"Neither do I," Therin replied, carving a path through the top of the frost covered table with his finger, the flakes of snow melting at his touch.

"How can something be too empty?" Belina stopped, turning back towards Dayne. She had the same look on her face as she did every time she thought she caught him out, that same glint in her eye. "It's either empty or it's not. It can't be *too* empty. You're either dead or you're not. You're never *too* dead."

"Belina, I will hurt you."

"Try it. You remember what happened at the Tower of Ilragorn, don't you? I'll put you on your back again."

"I swear to—"

"Will the two of you shut up?" Therin's voice didn't rise above a whisper, but it held such force it caused both Belina and Dayne to take a step back. "You're like bickering siblings. This isn't a game. My people are dying here. They are being locked away and chained while runes are carved into their flesh, consuming their souls from the inside out. Pull yourselves together or leave."

Therin stormed off down the corridor, at least as much as his graceful stride would allow. With the way his cloak drifted behind him, it was as if he were gliding.

Belina leaned in to Dayne, whispering, "He didn't mention the whole 'runes being carved in to flesh' thing before, didn't he not?"

Dayne shook his head, pulling his lips inward. "He did not."

"I didn't think so. I really wish he had mentioned that. I would have found Aeson myself." Pulling a knife from its sheath on her belt, Belina followed after Therin, muttering something incomprehensible as she did.

Dayne drew a deep breath in through his nose, letting it sit in his chest for a few moments before exhaling. No matter what lay ahead, he would keep pushing forward. This elf was the key to finding Sylvan Anura.

The group made their way to the end of the corridor and up a flight of stairs that led to the second storey of the bastion. Frost crunched with each step, echoing faintly off the walls, piercing the silence of the abandoned structure. He ran his hand along the stone rail of the balustrade, the settled snow melting at his touch. As his fingers moved along the stone, they slipped downward into a groove that had been hidden beneath the layer of icy white. Dayne brushed the snow away with his hand, revealing three jagged furrows carved into the stone. They looked like claw marks, too rough to have been made with a blade of any sort. "What in the gods happened here?" he whispered to himself.

"Hopefully we don't find out," Belina answered. "Come on."

Dayne frowned, casting his gaze over the furrows once more before nodding to Belina and carrying on up the stairs.

The second storey of the bastion was just as empty as the first. A few wooden benches and chairs coated in ice-crusted cobwebs lay scattered around, some resting against walls, others lying broken on the floor. Turning, Dayne followed the others up a second staircase that ascended to the third storey.

The staircase opened into a square chamber about fifty feet by fifty feet. The wall in front of the staircase was barren except for a torn tapestry that hung over itself, flapping in the unrelenting wind that tore through the mountains and rushed through the shattered windows of the bastion. The colours of the tapestry had faded over time, but the background looked as though it had once been a vivid red trimmed with gold. Rows of decrepit weapon racks ran along the two side walls, some empty, some holding rusted spears and swords.

Apart from the broken windows, the only source of light in the room came from the wide archway set into the wall behind the stairs, opening out to the battlements and on to the chasm-spanning bridge.

The icy rush of the mountain wind crashed into Dayne as he stepped beyond the bastion's protection and out onto the battlements. Above, the sunlight dwindled, slowly being replaced by the pale light of the crescent moon.

"Why did we decide to come now?" Belina asked, staring out across the wide stone bridge and up towards the gargantuan keep that lay set into the mountain on the other side. "I mean, this is creepy enough, but why did we come here as the sun is setting? Nothing good ever happens after dark. Mark my words."

Therin moved past Belina and Dayne, taking a few steps out onto the bridge before turning. "Afraid of the dark, Belina?"

"What idiot isn't afraid of the dark? Did you not hear me? *Nothing* good happens after dark. You're a storyteller. You, of all people, should know this. Tell me one happy story that takes place on a mountainside at night in an abandoned fortress."

Therin gave a weak smile, his silver hair coruscating in the fading light of the setting sun. "The people inside that keep can't wait for the sun to rise."

His cloak and hair flapping in the crosswind, Therin turned and set off across the bridge, the looming shadow of the keep slowly engulfing him.

Belina rested her hand on Dayne's shoulder. "How badly do you want to kill Sylvan Anura?"

Frowning, Dayne shook his head, then set off after Therin.

"Honestly," Belina called after him. "I'm sure she'll die of old age eventually."

Belina's words sounded as though they were nothing but an echo in the raging wind that battered the bridge, fading into the back of Dayne's mind. They may as well have been. He had one purpose: to get back to his family. To do that, Sylvan Anura needed to die, followed by Loren Koraklon. If the only way to make that happen was within the walls of that keep, then that's precisely where he was going. If he died, at least he would die knowing that he never stopped.

With each step across the bridge, the keep seemed to grow higher, its smooth stone walls rising in stark contrast to the rough rockface that surrounded it. Arched windows were set into the wall along the upper storeys of the keep, glass and wood long since shattered and broken, while a large doorway of dark metal inlaid with intricate patterns of tarnished gold sat at the front of the keep, breaking up the surface of smooth stone.

By the time Dayne reached Therin, the doors were ajar.

"It wasn't locked." The elf didn't turn to look at Dayne. Instead, his outstretched hand rested on the metal door, his gaze scanning its surface.

"Is that a good or a bad sign?"

"I'm not sure yet. But there's only one way to find out." Therin pushed the door open another foot or so, just wide enough for the three of them to enter, then stepped inside.

"Has he already gone in?" Belina asked as she stepped off the bridge. "Of course, he has. Fuck it. Let's go. The sooner we're done with this, the better." She placed her hand on Dayne's back and pushed him through the door.

Near complete darkness greeted Dayne as he stepped through the doorway. Slivers of cold moonlight passed through the shattered windows above, but they offered precious little light to illuminate the depths of the fortress before him.

A slight tingle was Dayne's only warning before a brilliant white light burst into existence, forcing Dayne to gasp and cover his eyes. In a panic, he pulled his arm away, desperate to see what stood before him. As the world slowly returned to focus and his eyes adjusted to the new light, shapes began to take form. Therin stood before him, a glowing white orb floating in the air at his side.

"Apologies," the elf said. "I should have thought before creating the baldír." As though reacting to Therin's words, the orb grew dimmer, taking the strain off Dayne's eyes.

"What is that?" The glowing orb pulsated, floating only a few feet from the ground. Dayne could see the threads of Air, Spirit, and Fire moving about the orb, holding it together, but he could not follow their patterns.

"I can teach you," Therin answered. "But I do not have time right now."

Dayne nodded, pulling his eyes from the baldír to examine the hallway in which they stood.

The floor consisted of slabs of grey stone dressed by a long carpet that Dayne was sure had once been grand and vibrant, but now held a dullish grey hue that mirrored the stone. The walls rose almost a hundred feet into the air, arching and meeting at the top. Thick columns were set into the walls about twenty feet apart, the tops of which were carved into intricate depictions of roaring lions. Dayne couldn't see how far the hallway stretched as the light from the baldír only forced the shadows back so far.

The brittle carpet cracked beneath his feet, the sounds bouncing off the walls as though he had broken glass. "Well, it's definitely not empty," he said, spotting multiple sets of boot prints pressed into the thin layer of frost that coated the floor.

"Damn, I was really holding out for that," Belina said, running her foot over one of the prints as she slipped another knife from its sheath.

"Keep quiet," Therin whispered. "Your voices will carry. Come."

"Keep quiet," Belina muttered as she passed Dayne, her voice taking on a mocking tone.

Dayne laughed, following after the others. But his laughter quickly faded as he moved down the barren hallway, shadows dancing across the floor as the baldír moved along beside Therin, its light ever shifting. Everything about the place set Dayne on edge. The darkness, the emptiness, the cold, the echoing sounds that bounced off the stone and high ceilings. But apart from that, something felt *wrong*. Like something watched him from the shadows, scratching at his mind, probing, trying to find a way inside. His mind recoiled at the sensation.

Before long, the corridor opened into a chamber that rose higher still, stretching another fifty or so feet towards a domed roof. About halfway up the walls, a balustrade framed balcony ran around the circumference of the chamber. A chill rippled over Dayne's skin as he looked towards the shadow-touched balcony. He dropped his hand to the pommel of his sword.

"What is it?" Therin whispered, following Dayne's gaze.

"I thought I saw something." Dayne tilted his head, leaning forward as he squinted, straining to see in the dim light.

"It may just be your mind playing tricks. I can feel it too. There's something off about this place. Something I've felt before."

"Felt before?"

"A long time ago. Come, we need to keep moving."

It took Dayne more than a few moments to pull his fingertips away from the pommel of his sword.

"Here," Belina called, her voice a hushed whisper. "This door's been used recently."

Dayne and Therin made their way over to Belina, who stood on the other side of the chamber by a metal doorway with a hexagonal top. Drag marks were evident on the floor beside the door, where the frost had been shifted from the opening and closing.

Glancing at the marks on the floor, Therin nodded, pulling a slightly curved sword from the sheath at his hip. By instinct, Dayne touched his fingertips against the pommels of his knives and sword, before reaching back and brushing his hand across the wood of his bow and the twenty-four goose-feather fletched arrows in his quiver. He shrugged his bow into his hands, following Therin through the doorway.

As soon as they stepped through, Therin released the baldír, letting its light fade from existence. Dayne was about to complain when he realised why. Before them lay a long corridor, at least twenty feet wide, tall enough for three men to stand atop one another. At the end of the corridor was what looked to be a large chamber, illuminated by a warm, orange, flickering glow. *Torches.*

Dropping low to the ground, Therin, Belina, and Dayne crept down the corridor. The sound of frost crunching underfoot was conspicuous only by its absence. Dayne hadn't noticed it at first, but this area of the keep felt warmer. The heat from the torches must have melted any frost that had previously clung to the stone.

At the end of the corridor was a landing fronted by a low wall that spread out to either side, overlooking a chamber that sat at least fifty feet below. A pair of staircases ran along the walls either side of the landing, descending to the chamber, where four guards in red steel plate stood watch. Two passageways were set into the wall on either side of the chamber, a pair of the guards stationed at each.

"Inquisition Praetorians," Therin whispered as he peered over the ledge of the wall.

Dayne wasn't entirely sure why, but it was almost comforting to the see the guards in their gleaming red plate. Whatever sensation it was that had set his hair on end was unnatural, sinister. But these were only men. He could fight men. He could kill men. "We need to take them quietly."

Belina nodded. "I'll go left. Count to one hundred. Therin, stay here."

Dayne could see the look of irritation on Therin's face as Belina stalked off, making her way down the staircase to the left.

"Let us do what you brought us here to do," Dayne whispered before creeping down the staircase to the right, keeping his head below the line of the wall. *Twenty-seven.* He could feel the beat of his heart pulsing in his veins, his chest fluttering.

Four hundred and seventy-nine. That was how many lives he had taken since meeting Belina. He had not found peace in a single death, not even the slightest of joys. Though any man who took joy in killing was a man worth killing. Even so, he would have thought that, with time, it would come easier. But it never did, particularly not like this – his blood, cold in his veins, his targets entirely unaware of their looming death. Even that word; he used it so soullessly: *targets.* They were people, flesh and blood. But it was a choice between them and his family.

They would not leave this place alive. *Sixty-three.*

Dayne pulled two throwing knives from the strap across his chest, the cold touch of steel familiar against his fingertips. The end of the staircase was only a few paces away. *Seventy-five.*

Reaching the last bend in the stairs, he drew a deep breath into his lungs, letting his muscles relax. *Eighty-three.*

The Praetorians were only a few feet away, their red plate seeming to glow an incandescent orange in the light of the torches. He could hear them talking.

"Where are you going first when we rotate off?" one of the guards asked the other.

Ninety.

Just as Dayne was readying to release his first knife, the other guard responded.

"My sister had a kid last week. A boy. I haven't gotten to see him yet. I only opened the letter before we left, but I'll go there first, I think."

Dayne froze, his hand trembling. Images flashed through his mind of Alina, screaming, calling for him. Stormwatch burning. Him leaving. He had never wanted to leave. *I never wanted to leave you alone…*

Thump. Thump. The sound of Belina's knives lodging in the other two guards' throats. Dayne shook his head, his balance shifting, his eyes widening. He looked up. The two Praetorians before him had drawn their swords. They had seen him.

Hesitation leads to lives lost. Marlin's voice echoed in the back of his mind

Recovering, Dayne launched his knife, and then a second, as quick as his hand could move. The first knife caught the Praetorian on the left, slicing through the links of mail that protected his neck. Blood sprayed. The man fell, clutching his throat. Dayne reached out to the Spark, quieting the man's landing with threads of Air.

The second Praetorian lifted his arm just in time to catch the knife mid-flight, sending it ricocheting behind him, clanging against the wall. He charged, but before he could reach Dayne, a glint of steel flashed in the air. A blade plunged into the man's eye, sliding through the narrow slits in his helm. The man stumbled, falling to one knee, howling. Panic slithered through Dayne's veins, his heart beating erratically, his brain still foggy from the flashing memories. Therin glided past him, taking the man's head from his shoulders in one sweep of his curved blade, blood spurting.

And then it was over.

What just happened? Dayne's chest trembled as he dragged in breath. He could still feel his heart pounding like horse hooves on clay, his mouth dry as cotton.

"Are you hurt?"

Dayne looked up to see Therin extending a hand, the curiosity in his eyes mixing with a touch of understanding.

Dayne grabbed the elf's hand, dragging himself to his feet. "I'm fine. I didn't need your help."

Therin responded with a weak smile and the slightest of nods, but no words.

Belina strode over, wiping the blood from her knives with the sleeves of her coat. She stopped, her eyes taking in the scene. The two dead Praetorians. Therin helping

Dayne to his feet. Dayne readied himself for a witty remark or comment, but none came. Her eyes said only one thing: *Are you all right?*

Dayne nodded. He was fine. At least, he thought he was fine. That had never happened before. He'd never frozen like that. It was like he had no control over his limbs or his mind. It was… terrifying.

"Which way do we go?" Belina said, pushing over one of the dead Praetorians with her foot so he lay on his back. She looked up at Therin.

"Two possible paths." Steel glinted as Therin flipped a small, round-backed knife across his fingers. "We should split up. You and Dayne take—"

"No." Belina crossed her arms, shaking her head, her two knives still clutched firmly in her fists.

"No?" Therin tilted his head.

"No." Belina shrugged, as she always did. "I let you take us into this place as night fell, but I'd rather drag my bare arse across hot coals than split up down here. That is how we will die. We pick one way, and then we go together."

"But how do we—"

Belina held up her hand, cutting Therin off once more. The annoyance was visible on the elf's face. But if Dayne knew one thing about Belina, it was that she didn't care in the slightest.

Without speaking, Belina walked back towards the other passageway. Once there, she stood for a few moments, turned, and walked back. She strode past Dayne and Therin, stood by the second passageway and then drew in a long breath through her nose. After a few moments, she nodded. "This way."

"What? Why?" Therin looked genuinely curious.

"Well," Belina said, puffing out her chest. "That passage-way over there smelled of sweat and slightly overcooked lamb. While this passageway smelled of genuine shit."

Both Dayne and Therin just stared at her.

"Must I always explain everything?" Belina paused for a moment, as though she had genuinely posed a question to which she expected an answer. "Fine. You're looking for prisoners, right? Well, are you more likely to be feeding the prisoners lamb or letting them sleep in their own shit? Well… that might not be lamb. It might be elf. I wouldn't know what elf smelled like. I—"

"*Belina.*" Dayne didn't have to say anything else.

"Right. Apologies." Belina raised both her hands, looking towards Therin. "It's *most likely* not elf… probably."

Dayne shook his head, resting his hand on Therin's shoulder. "Sorry."

"Where are you going?" Belina called out as Dayne set off down the passageway closest to them.

"Following the smell of shit."

Cast iron sconces lined the walls of the passageway, each bearing a thick white candle that burned with an orange glow. The sconces were set just far enough apart so their light didn't truly overlap, casting flickering shadows across the stone.

Dayne's pulse quickened as he approached the end of the passageway. His heart thumped against his ribs, the shockwaves rippling through his veins. Ahead, Dayne could see a chamber lit only by a few scattered sconces and the residual glow of the passageway's candles. The smell Belina had mentioned grew ever stronger the closer they got to the chamber, growing thick, palpable. It snaked through his nostrils and clogged the back of his throat. He had smelled it before, but never this strong: death. The hairs on his neck and arms pricked, that eerie feeling rushing across his skin. There was something wrong with this place. Something he'd never felt before. It was the same feeling that probed at him since they had first stepped foot in the bastion, scratching at his mind, trying to get inside.

He felt a hand rest on his shoulder.

"Together," Belina whispered, nodding.

Dayne nodded back, tightening his fingers around the handle of his sword. "Therin, could you cast a baldír again?"

Almost immediately, Dayne felt Therin reaching out to the Spark, weaving thin threads of Fire, Air, and Spirit together, forming tiny fragments of light that coalesced into a small orb that emitted a dim, white light.

"I dare not make it any brighter," the elf said, stepping past Dayne, into the chamber, the baldír floating beside him. "If there are any mages nearby, they may sense the threads."

Dayne nodded, his eyes following the baldír, watching as it pulsed light. He thought he could pick out the threads Therin had used, replicate them. It would take some trying, but he was fairly confident.

"What is this place?" Belina asked, covering her nose and mouth with the back of her hand, her fingers still wrapped around the handles of her knives. She ran a finger along the top of a long wooden bench that stood beside the passageway's entrance. "No dust…"

"Here," Therin whispered.

Therin stood before a cell barred by latticed iron. With his eyes adjusting to the darkness, Dayne saw that the chamber held many more cells just like it, stretching off into the shadows.

"Is there anyone…" Dayne looked into the cell, his voice trailing off. Partially illuminated by the white glow of the baldír was an emaciated shape that looked as though it had once been an elf. Now, though, it was nothing more than a husk, the skin blackened, dry and brittle, stretched over bones to the point of cracking. Cuts and marks covered the body, some almost looking as though they were carved into a particular shape. Nausea coiled in Dayne's stomach, threatening to turn it. He covered his mouth, holding his breath until the feeling subsided.

"May Heraya embrace you," Belina whispered, her gaze fixed on the withered corpse. In the dim light, Dayne couldn't be sure, but it looked as though a tear had formed in the corner of Belina's eye. "Nobody should die like this…"

Dayne felt Therin draw from the Spark, pushing threads of Air through the door's lock. *Click.*

Therin pulled open the iron-barred door, summoning creaks and screeches from the age-worn metal. He knelt beside the dead elf, resting his hand on their cheek. "Du vyin alura anis."

"What did you say?" Dayne asked as Therin pulled himself to his feet.

"I told her she can rest now." The elf looked back at the body that lay broken on the floor, his hand clenching into a fist. "Whoever did this will pay with their lives."

Many of the other cells were empty, but even more held the same sight: elven corpses, emaciated and broken, markings carved into their skin.

"What are those markings?" Dayne asked, looking over the body of one of the elves.

"Blood runes," Therin replied, brushing his fingers across one of the runes carved into the dead elf's chest. "Whatever they are doing here, it must be stopped."

Dayne almost leapt from his skin as a sound echoed from further up the chamber. Belina flashed him a glance, moving forward towards the sound. Therin and Dayne followed.

A cough sounded, hoarse and weak. "Anyone?"

Dayne didn't have a chance to say anything before Therin broke into a sprint towards the voice, dashing past Belina.

By the time Dayne and Belina caught up to him, Therin was kneeling within one of the cells, a sick-looking creature on the edge of death in his arms, curled up like a cat. It was an elf, small in body, its bones protruding through its skin, threatening to break the surface. Patches of brittle hair sprouted from atop the elf's head, and its eyes were bloodshot.

"Please…" the elf muttered, their voice distorted and cracked. "Please make it end…" The poor creature rocked itself back and forth in Therin's lap, its spine visible through the parchment-thin skin. "The voices… the pain… I can't…"

Dayne stood there, speechless, pain twisting in his heart. *What kind of nightmare is this?* Even Belina looked as though her heart was being pulled from her chest.

"Du vyin alura anis." Therin reached his hand into his coat, producing the same round-backed knife Dayne had seen him flipping across his fingers earlier. With only the slightest of hesitations, he drove the knife through the soft tissue at the side of the elf's head. As if reacting to the blade, a red glow shone across the floor where Therin knelt, seeming to come from the twisted elf he held in his arms. The glow only lasted a few moments before it flickered, eventually fading from existence.

Therin lay the elf's body on the floor with as much care as a mother swaddling a babe, then rose to his feet and slammed his fists against the cell wall. "Gods damn it!" His voice dropped from a roar to a fragile melancholy. "What kind of monsters would do this?"

To Dayne's surprise, Belina stepped into the cell, resting her hand on Therin's shoulder. "He is at peace now. Nobody can hurt him anymore."

Therin turned, nodding absently, a tear running down his cheek, pooling at his chin. He clasped his hand behind Belina's head, pulling their foreheads together. "Thank you," he whispered, before kneeling beside the child. Carefully, he turned the body onto its back.

Dayne held back a gasp at the sight of an enormous marking carved into the child's chest, smaller markings carved all around it. Again, images of Alina flashed across his mind. *"I need you…"* Alina's voice echoed. He shook his head, clasping his hand to his temple. *Snap out of it, Dayne.*

"I've only ever seen these rune markings carved by Urak Shamans." Therin ran his fingers along the ridges of torn flesh in the child's chest.

More sounds began to echo down the chamber, shifting bodies, weak voices. Dayne and Belina exchanged a glance while Therin got to his feet, stepping from the cell.

"Can it be undone?" Dayne asked, following after Therin.

Therin shook his head. "I don't believe so. I know very little of blood magic, but it has long been suspected that these rune markings feed on the Essence of the bearer, consuming them. In the case of the Urak Bloodmarked, the runes grant them immense power, twisting their bodies, draining their Essence in return. These look more like… experiments."

Therin rested his hand on the barred doors of the next cell, the light from the baldír revealing another elf huddled in the corner, her bony knees pulled to her chest. She looked like something pulled from the depths of a nightmare. Her eyes were sunken, a reddish glow seeming to pulsate behind them. Small, intricate runes glowing with a dim, red light were carved along her arms and legs, which had taken on an almost scaled appearance. The rune-marked elf snarled, baring what few teeth remained in her mouth, froth foaming at the corners of her lips.

They found many more like her in the other cells, varying runes carved into their skin in different positions and sizes. For every one they found alive, they found five more dead. And those that were alive seemed no better off. There had to have been hundreds of cells.

"Why would anyone do this?" Dayne whispered, more to himself than anyone else. He dropped onto his haunches, looking through the bars of a cell at an elf whose legs had withered and transformed into twisted leathery things more like claws than anything else. She was still alive, but then… she also wasn't. Her eyes were open so wide it looked as though someone was pulling back her lids. Where her eyes should have been white, they glowed with a pulsating red light just as the runes on her legs. She didn't blink; she just stared, her head twitching side to side.

"Over here," Belina called, her voice devoid of its usual cocksure tone. "Uraks…"

The cell Belina stood before held two bodies, one massive, and one no bigger than a human child of one or two summers. They were Uraks for certain. But that wasn't what stood out to Dayne. They weren't emaciated and twisted. They almost looked healthy, as though this had happened only recently.

"They're dead," Therin announced after opening the cell and kneeling beside the bodies, checking for signs of life. "This one is only a newborn. The cord is still attached. Likely dead before birth."

Dayne had never thought he could hold sympathy for Uraks. But as he looked down over the mother and child, his heart twisted in on itself and his throat constricted.

"There are no runes," Therin continued, running his hand over the mother's arm, a mix of confusion and curiosity in his voice.

"Therin, what is happening here?" Dayne couldn't take his eyes from the two bodies. "We need to know what you aren't telling us."

"I know what you know," Therin replied, lifting himself to his feet. Despite the calm that radiated from the elf's voice, Dayne could see the profound sense of loss in his eyes, in the way his shoulders sagged and his breath trembled. "Efialtír looms over this place. His influence hides in every crack and crevice. His whispers are thick in the air. You can hear them, Dayne, in the back of your mind."

Without even a question, Dayne knew precisely what Therin was speaking of: that feeling probing at him, scratching, trying to break in.

"In places where blood magic is used frequently," Therin continued. "The veil between worlds can grow thin. Efialtír's touch can corrupt and warp minds. Whatever is being done here is being done in his name, and it ends tonight."

"Agreed," Dayne said.

Belina nodded, but the look of concern on her face as she stared at the two bodies caused Dayne's heart to ache. She had been unsettled ever since Elkenrim. Ever since her father.

Dayne and Belina followed Therin as he stepped from the cell and made his way down the chamber, casting his eyes into every cell they passed along the way.

So many of them…

At the end of the corridor was an enormous set of double doors. Solid oak beams reinforced with riveted bands of iron. They stretched almost to the ceiling and were wide enough to fit three wagons side by side.

"What do we do about the survivors?" Dayne asked Therin, gesturing back towards the cells.

"When this is done, we release them." The way the elf lingered on the word 'release' told Dayne that he did not mean from the cells. "That is all we can do for them now."

Swallowing hard, Dayne nodded. It had been a while since he had felt true fear. That gut twisting, hollow-chest, hands trembling kind of fear. He didn't fear death. At least, he didn't fear the pain of it. But the thought of ending up like those elves shook him to his core. When he was younger, he had often wondered what the phrase 'a fate worse than death' meant. But now he understood.

"Last chance to turn back."

Dayne and Therin both glared at Belina, who held her arms up in surrender. "Yeah, I didn't think that was going to be an option. All right, let's go. We all have to die sometime."

With one last look towards Belina, Therin leaned forward and pushed the door open.

VII

BLOODMARKED

Four figures stood at the centre of the chamber atop a raised stone dais. Three were men, two with red cloaks draped over their shoulders – Inquisitors – and one with black – a Battlemage. The fourth figure was a woman, her dark hair tied in a knot at the back of her head, garbed in grey robes over leather: a Scholar. Before them were three elves, their wrists and ankles bound to large metal platforms that were tilted vertically. Two of the elves were alive, if barely, but the third, on the rightmost platform, looked as though he had been starved and trampled by a horse. His limbs were twisted and broken, shattered bones piercing through the skin around his knees and forearms. Runes had been carved all over the elf's body, his skin almost entirely stained crimson from the dried blood.

One of the Inquisitors was examining the dead elf while the Scholar leaned over a large leather-bound book that rested atop a wooden stand, her hand moving quickly from side to side, a pen gripped in her fingers.

The chamber itself stretched almost two hundred feet wide and even more across, its walls rising to an arched roof supported by buttresses and thick stone columns. Cast iron sconces were set into the columns, washing the chamber in an orange-red light.

Dayne counted fourteen Lorian soldiers in total, including six Praetorians, the orange-red light of the sconces shimmering off their burnished red plate. Five stood beside the cells on the eastern wall, one between each cell, swords at their hips, shields slung across their backs. The other nine stood at the foot of the dais, including all six Praetorians, thick shafted spears gripped in their fists, axes hanging from weapon belts.

Not one of the chamber's occupants seemed to notice Dayne, Belina, and Therin slipping through the doorway and crouching behind two of the columns that framed the entrance.

"What's the plan?" Belina whispered, peering around the column, knives still gripped in her fists. "I count four mages and thirteen soldiers, six Praetorians among them."

"Fourteen soldiers," Dayne corrected.

"Still, good odds." There wasn't a hint of sarcasm in Belina's voice. They had faced far worse on many an occasion. But Dayne didn't like the idea of facing down four Lorian mages. Belina turned to Therin. "Any suggestions?"

Before Therin could answer, a blood-chilling shriek ripped through the chamber. The sound sent a shiver rippling through Dayne, his stomach twisting. Up on the dais, one of the Inquisitors had begun to carve runes into the elf on the middle platform. The shrieks were like nothing Dayne had ever heard. Pure agony, as though the elf's soul was being rent along with their skin. As the Inquisitor sliced his blade through the elf's flesh, the hilt of the dagger in his hand began to pulsate with a vivid red glow.

"We kill them all." Therin pulled his curved sword from its scabbard and strode from behind the column, reaching out for the Spark, fury burning in his eyes. The sheer power that radiated from the elf thrummed through the air, threads of Fire, Spirit, and Air whirling around him. Striding towards the dais, Therin held out his hand, streaks of blue lightning surging from his fingertips, cracking against the stone floor before tearing through the Inquisitor who had been carving the runes. The Inquisitor collapsed in a lifeless heap on the dais, smoke drifting from his charred body.

The other mages turned, shock etched into their faces. Dayne slipped his bow from his back, nocking an arrow, scanning the chamber one last time. *Six Praetorians, nine guards, three mages.* The Scholar and the remaining Inquisitor were still standing by the dead elf, their feet planted. The Battlemage stood to the left, his gaze shifting from the body of his fallen companion to Therin. Dayne felt the mage begin to reach out to the Spark. He needed to take the man down before that happened.

Dayne drew back his bow, feeling the tension build in the string, his muscles pulling reflexively. *One more step on the path. I'm almost home. One more step.* He lifted his fingers, loosing the arrow, nocking a second arrow even before the tip of the first had plunged into the side of the Battlemage's head. The man stumbled sideways as though hit by nothing more than a stone, a look of shock on his face. He held for a moment, then collapsed in a heap, motionless. Shouts rose about the chamber, the clink of metal boots on stone.

Dayne loosed a second arrow, but the Inquisitor it was intended for turned just in time. The arrow collided with a thread of Air, skittering harmlessly against the ground. Dayne felt the air change. Both the surviving mages were pulling from the Spark, as was Therin.

Dayne had never been in a room with so many mages before. He had always been taught to hide his affinity, to shield it from those who would seek to control it. He used it only when he needed to. Now, however, as its influence seeped into the air, it was almost as though the Spark was calling to him, urging him to draw from it.

"Keep them away from Therin!" Belina flashed past Dayne, sword in one hand, knife in the other, her feet eating the ground towards the dais.

Take the strongest first. Pivoting, Dayne nocked and loosed two arrows into the thick of soldiers at the front of the dais who were now charging towards Therin. One Praetorian crashed to the ground, the arrow slamming into his neck, blood spraying. A second stumbled, dropping to their knees before collapsing on their side. The arrow punched into the plate that protected their chest – not an instant kill, but they wouldn't be rising again. Dayne charged, loosing one more arrow as he did, before slinging his bow across his back. A third Praetorian dropped, the arrow passing through the slits of their helmet.

Dayne ripped his sword from its scabbard, reaching out to the Spark. He pulled on threads of Earth, feeling them drag through his mind, coarse as sand, solid as stone. The smell of loam filled his nostrils. Allowing the Spark to flow through him, he funnelled the threads into the floor, letting them seep through the stone beneath the charging soldiers. Then, just as he was within striking distance, he clenched his left fist, cracking the stone. Fissures spread through the surface of the floor. Shouts rose as the soldiers lost their footing, tripping over raised ridges of stone, stumbling through cracks as Therin glided past them towards the dais.

Do not hesitate, do not contemplate mercy. Marlin Arkon's words.

Dayne drew in a deep breath, tightened his grip on the hilt of his sword, then pushed off his back foot, launching himself into the group of staggering Lorians.

He crashed into the first soldier, knocking the man off balance. Twisting his back foot, Dayne drove his sword upward through the man's neck, pulling it free, using the momentum to swing himself around, his blade colliding with a Praetorian's spear tip that was meant to take his head. Swinging his sword back around, Dayne carried his blade down, cleaving the soldier's arm at the elbow before driving the sword through her gut, feeling the grate as steel dragged against steel. The woman howled, Dayne pulling his blade free, blood sluicing from the wound. The screams faded into the back of his mind, the fever of battle taking over. *I am the blade.*

He moved swiftly, weaving between the soldiers and Praetorians, not allowing them even a moment to recover, hammering them with threads of Air, driving steel through their flesh as they stumbled. They were well trained, but he was Valtaran, and he wielded the power of the Spark.

The soldiers who had guarded the eastern cells had reached the dais. Belina sliced through them, her hands a whir of steel.

Flashes of light erupted from the dais, screams. Dayne turned, catching sight of Therin's blade cleaving through the neck of the remaining Inquisitor, the ground around them scorched and smoking.

A streak of pain ripped through Dayne's side, forcing him to release his grip on his sword. He howled, steel clattering against the stone. As fast as his hand could move, he slipped a knife from the strap across his chest, twisted, and drove the blade down through the slits in his attacker's helm, calling forth a stream of blood and clear fluid. Letting go of the handle, Dayne lifted his hand, then slammed the flat of his palm down on the knife's pommel, driving the blade deeper into the man's skull. The Praetorian's body shuddered, then went limp. Dayne grasped the shaft of the man's spear, ripping it free from his dying grip.

The smooth wood of the spear felt at home in his hands. It was oak, not the ash wood of a valyna, but it would take a life just as well.

Spinning, he cracked the butt of the spear against a charging soldier's helm, feeling the vibrations resonate through the wooden shaft. Shifting his feet, he flipped the spear and drove the blade through the man's neck, splitting the links of his mail, spilling his blood onto the stone floor. Only one soldier and one Praetorian remained, both moving to circle him.

Dayne reached out to the Spark once more, surging towards the Praetorian on his right. The woman struck her spear towards Dayne's chest. Dayne twisted, shifting his own spear into his right hand as the Praetorian's slid past him, slicing through the fabric of his coat and grazing the leather beneath. Bringing his left hand down, he swung the butt of his spear upward, slamming it into the underside of the Praetorian's jaw before ramming it into her throat with as much force as he could muster. He heard the distinct sound of bone breaking. The soldier crashed to the ground, her hands clasped to her mail-clad throat.

Pulling from the Spark, Dayne launched thick threads of air towards the last remaining soldier, sending the man careening through the chamber, crashing into the base of a column, body going limp.

Dayne's chest heaved, his heart pounding, his lungs dragging in air. He could feel the Spark sapping him, draining the strength from his bones as it always did when he drew too much. He turned to the soldier who lay on the ground, her throat crushed. Raising his spear, he drove the blade down through the woman's plate, feeling the resistance, then pushing through. The soldier's eyes bulged, her body twitching. Dayne pushed harder. The twitching stopped.

Pulling his spear free, Dayne turned to find Therin standing with his foot on the Scholar's neck, threads of Air holding the mage in place, threads of Spirit weaving through her body, encasing her. Blood dripped from the length of Therin's curved blade, bodies lying lifeless on the ground around him.

Only a foot or so to Therin's right, Belina pulled her knife free of an imperial soldier's throat, pushing the body away as it slumped to the floor. Sweat glistened on her skin, she limped slightly on her right leg, and blood dripped from a cut at the side of her head.

"What is this place?" Therin roared down at the Scholar, a fury burning in his eyes, veins bulging on his neck. The elf had seemed the epitome of calm up to that point. But what they had seen in this keep could have turned the steadiest of hands to bloody murder.

"Dayne, a little help?"

Reluctantly, Dayne pulled his gaze from Therin and the Scholar, turning to find Belina standing beside the elf who lay on the middle platform, cutting through the leather straps that bound the poor wretch in place. The elf was still screaming, tears carving through weeks' worth of dirt and grime, blood streaking from the runes the Inquisitor had carved into her chest. With the last of the bindings cut, the elf slumped into Belina's arms, sobbing and twitching. Belina lowered the elf to the ground and laid her against the base of the metal platform. She turned to Dayne, nodding towards the last elf, who lay unconscious on the third platform, wrists and ankles bound. "Cut him down."

Dayne nodded. He lay the spear on the ground and pulled a knife from its sheath, slicing through the leather bonds that held the elf in place. The elf fell forwards, collapsing into Dayne's arms, mumbling incoherently, his eyes glazed over. He was only a child, and he looked even younger than Alina had when Dayne left.

Dayne lay the elf on the floor, resting him beside his companion. "It's all right," he said, placing his hands against the elf's cheeks. *How could the empire do this to children?* "You're safe now. We've got you."

Reluctantly, he left the child to their sobbing and rose to his feet. "Therin, we need to go. We don't know how many more of them are here, and these two are in a bad way."

"We'll go when I'm done!" Therin roared back, not taking his eyes from the Scholar who lay trapped beneath his foot. "Tell me, now! What are you doing to my people?"

The woman coughed and spluttered, blood spraying over her bottom lip, her hands flat against the ground, bound by threads of Air. She was laughing. "You do not scare me, elf. The Saviour will take me into his arms. The Chosen will be called. There is *nothing* you can do. Your kin died for a higher purpose. They should be proud."

"Efialtír is no saviour," Therin growled. "He is The Traitor, the great deceiver, the devourer of souls." Dayne felt Therin draw deeper from the Spark, pulling on thick threads of Earth and Spirit.

What is he doing?

"You *will* talk." Therin tilted his head sideways, his eyes cold, measuring. "And you *will* feel pain for what you did here. The sooner you talk, the sooner I will release you from your misery."

Therin funnelled the threads of Earth and Air into the mage's body. Dayne watched as the threads sunk into the mage's skin, coiling around her limbs like snakes. The mage let out a chilling scream, her body convulsing, blood-tinted foam forming at the corners of her mouth.

"Speak!" Veins bulged in Therin's neck, his chest trembling, his boot pressing down on the mage's neck.

Dayne looked to Belina, who knelt beside the two elves. She shook her head. Dayne knew what she meant – *don't do it.*

Dayne ignored her. "Therin, this is not the way. Not like this."

Therin rounded on Dayne, cold fury in his eyes. But it wasn't his stare that unsettled Dayne. It was the calmness in his voice. "For what she has done here, I would shatter her bones and not think twice. There is no pain she could bear that would balance the scales. When you have seen the centuries I have, then you can think to question my judgement."

Therin's eyes bored through Dayne, daring him to challenge. The sheer power that radiated from the elf rippled through the air like lightning, threads of Earth and Air swirling around him.

"I think I know what they were doing here." Belina's voice sheared through the tension-thick air. She stood by a wooden stand that held a thick, leather-bound book – the one the Scholar had been writing in. Belina ran her finger across the page, reading the words aloud. *"Subject four hundred and fifty-three. Male. Elf. Fifteen summers. Result: deceased. Note – the results of this runeset seem promising. Subject four hundred and fifty-three showed increased aggression and strength, lasting four days longer than the previous subject before expiration. Though it seems the elven constitution is not as suited to the gift as that of the Uraks, I maintain strong belief that this is the path to the Chosen. Sufficient information has been gathered to progress to the next stage. Subjects four hundred and fifty-four, four hundred and fifty-five, and four hundred and fifty-six will be trialled. The remaining subjects are to be terminated."*

Silence hung in the air as Belina's words trailed off. Therin stared down at the Scholar, his chest rising and falling in heavy sweeps, power radiating from him in pulses of rippling energy. "You sacrificed them to try and create Bloodmarked…" His voice didn't rise higher than a whisper, but pure hatred seeped through every word. "You tortured them. You twisted their bodies and burned their souls." Therin lifted his foot from the woman's neck, threads of Air still holding her in place. He knelt beside her, placing his hand on her shoulder. "You are nothing. Nobody will ever remember you. I will burn this place to the ground. May The Mother leave your soul to float adrift in the void."

With a visceral roar, Therin's power surged through the threads of Earth and Air that coiled around the Scholar. A physical shockwave erupted from the elf, crushing the mage's body, cracking the stone beneath her. The force of the blast swept vibrations through the stone, releasing plumes of stone dust from the roof. The woman's screams rose to a pitch that turned Dayne's stomach. But he forced himself to watch. If she had been Sylvan Anura, he would have done the same thing. This woman had earned every drop of pain that Therin poured into her. She had violated these elves. Torn them to pieces.

With one last pulse of energy, the mage's chest collapsed inwards, her arms and legs twisted, bones snapping and tearing through her skin. In an instant, her screams were gone, remembered only by the echo that lingered in the air like a ghost.

Therin knelt over the woman, his chest heaving, his jaw clenched. Slowly, Dayne felt Therin release the Spark, the threads of Earth and Air fading from existence. The elf lifted his hand from the mage's shattered body, blood and bits of bone smeared across his skin. He stumbled sideways, Dayne catching him beneath the arms before he fell.

"I'm fine." Therin pushed Dayne away, his voice only an absent whisper as though he was talking not to Dayne, but to himself. Grunting, he dropped to his knees beside the two elves who lay on the metal platforms. The child looked relatively unharmed, if a little bruised and malnourished, but the other elf was not so lucky. Her chest was a mess of knotted flesh, blood seeping from the runes carved into her skin. Therin ran his hand along a jagged rune carved just below the elf's collarbone. "What have they done to you, my child?"

Belina moved to touch Therin's shoulder, but Dayne shook his head. Belina must have seen the sorrow in his eyes, for she pulled back her hand, a grim look of recognition on her face.

After a few moments, Therin rose to his feet, his eyes wet with tears, his hands shaking. "Help me release the others from their pain and take these two from this place. Then I will take you to Aeson. You have earned this and more, Dayne Ateres." Therin grasped Dayne's forearm. The tears that had been welling at the corner of his eyes began to fall, rolling down his cheeks in steady streams.

Dayne nodded. Releasing Therin's grasp, he knelt beside the elven child, took a deep breath, and scooped him up into his arms. Dayne could feel the child's chest rise and fall, dragging ragged breaths into his tired lungs. "It's all right," he whispered. "You're safe now."

PART 4

THE PATH TO HEALING

TWO WEEKS LATER

VIII

THE EMPTINESS OF TIME AND BLOOD

An island twenty miles east of Driftstone, Veloran Ocean
Year 3075 after doom

Dayne stood at the bow of the ship, his hands resting on the rail, fingers curling around the rough, damp wood. The familiar ocean spray was cool against his cheeks and the setting sun warm on his back, painting the waters ahead with brush strokes of vibrant orange. An island sat amidst the incandescent waters, a blotch of green and grey against the coruscating blues and oranges. The island was only a few miles wide, shaped like a three-quarter moon with hills that rose around the edges, descending towards the centre. Dayne could already see languid streaks of grey smoke rising from a house that sat atop the easternmost hill. At the foot of the hill, where the land tapered towards the water, a long pier jutted from a beach of grey sand and stones, the waves gently beating at its wooden legs.

"Are you all right?"

Dayne hadn't heard Belina approach. But then again, he never did; the woman moved like a whisper in the wind. "No." Dayne dug his fingernails into the damp rail, closing his eyes for a moment. Blotched colour painted the darkness behind his eyelids as though he had stared too long at the sun. "No, I'm not."

"You've waited five years for this, Dayne." Belina rested her hand on Dayne's shoulder.

"I've waited seven years, Belina."

"But did your life truly start before you met me? I mean, look at me."

Dayne lifted his head, unable to stop the smile that pulled at the corners of his mouth. Against his better judgment, he laughed. "You are a curse I can't seem to get rid of."

"I'm the curse that brought you here."

"That you are…" Dayne looked into Belina's dark brown eyes. "That, you are." Dayne pulled Belina into a tight embrace, wrapping his arms around her, nestling his chin against the crook of her neck.

"Anything to get close to my tits," she whispered in his ear.

"Fuck off, Belina." Dayne pulled away, still laughing, and leaned across the rail of the ship. "You have to ruin everything, don't you?"

Belina rested her forearms against the rail, rubbing her shoulder against Dayne's, her voice soft and low. "Whatever we find on that island, wherever Aeson tells us we must go to find Sylvan, I'm with you."

Dayne stared ahead, lost in the brilliant lights of the sparkling waves. "Our deal was for you to get me here.

You've done that. It might have taken you five years, but you did what you promised."

"And *you* did what *you* promised. Now, are you going to make me say it?"

"I sure am."

Belina sighed, shaking her head. Dayne didn't look at her, but he knew she was looking at him. "We're family, Dayne."

Dayne shifted his forearms on the rail, turning to Belina, raising his eyebrows. "Sorry, what did you say? I couldn't hear you. You were whispering."

Belina clasped her hands at the sides of Dayne's head and pulled their foreheads together. "We have spilled blood together. We have sent souls into the void. We have crossed thousands of miles by land and water. I have listened to you pine over Mera like a lovesick puppy, and we have shit in the same hole in the ground more times than I'm comfortable with." Dayne laughed as Belina shrugged, shaking her head as though trying to loose the memory. "You are my brother, Dayne. If not by birth, then by blood. Your fight is my fight."

Dayne's chest tightened at the words. For all her faults – and there were many, so, so many – Belina had been there for him. He lifted his hands to the back of Belina's head. When this was all over, he would bring her to meet Alina and Baren. They were her family now too. "Belina, I—"

A swift punch to the gut knocked the wind from Dayne's lungs, causing him to double over, coughing as he tried to breathe. Belina caught him, wrapping her hand around the back of his head, and whispered into his ear, "That's for making me say it."

Pushing Dayne back against the rail, Belina strode off down the ship, skipping past the oarsmen before throwing him a wink and dropping herself onto a bench that lay across the stern, leaning back to take in the sun. The woman was insane by all measures of the word. She was irrational, brash, completely unpredictable, her perception of what was acceptable was the opposite to any reasonable person's, and she had killed more people than she had eaten warm meals. And yet, he would die for her.

When he was younger, Dayne remembered asking his mother what love was. He had asked because every time Mera was near him, he had felt a tightness in his chest, his mouth went dry, and he stumbled over his words. Surely that had meant he was in love, he thought. But to be sure, he asked his mother, for she knew everything.

"Love, my son, cannot be quantified by how and why. It is the intangible tether that connects your heart to others. It holds no conditions or rules, for if it did, it would not be love, but simply convenience. It is not found in the 'because', it is found in the 'and yet'. Your father is strong, compassionate, and understanding, but it is not because of those things that I love him. Rather, they are why I admire him. He is also foolhardy, pig-headed, and he always says the wrong things. And yet, I love him anyway."

For a long time, Dayne hadn't understood what his mother had meant. He had nodded and smiled, feigning understanding. But through Belina, he had finally learned the meaning of his mother's words. He did not love Belina in the way his mother had loved his father, or in the way that he was now certain he loved Mera, but he did love her.

Pulling his gaze from Belina, Dayne looked to the starboard side of the ship, where Therin sat with his back against the rail, the two elves they had rescued sitting with him. The elder of the two sat to Therin's right, a linen shirt covering the scarred, knotted flesh that marred her chest. She looked brighter with the dirt, grime, and blood cleaned from her skin. But Dayne could still see the darkness in her eyes. Her long, blonde hair was thin and brittle, and her right hand shook with a persistent tremor. The mage hadn't finished the rune carving, and so Therin had been able to heal most of her wounds – at least the ones that could be seen with the naked eye. It had taken a few days, but eventually she spoke. Not to Dayne or Belina, only to Therin, and in a language that Dayne didn't understand, but it was a start.

Sitting across from them, his legs pulled to his chest, the side of his head resting on the tops of his knees, was the child. His face was gaunt, dark circles under his eyes, lips cracked. His body was so starved of food it looked as though his skin had been stretched too thin over fragile bones. He wore a long, linen shirt that was far too big, along with trousers held up by a length of tied rope. Not a single word had passed his lips.

It had been just over two weeks, and images of those cells still plagued Dayne's mind. He could still smell the fetor of death in his nostrils, the putrid aroma of vomit and voided bowls, the metallic tinge of blood, and the acrid stench of charred skin. Of all the elves in that keep, only the two before him could be saved. They had searched every cell and found three hundred and fifty-two elves, along with a pit full of charred bones, likely burned to lessen the stench of decay. Two hundred and sixty-six dead, eighty-six alive, though alive was a strong word. They were broken and twisted, their minds consumed. Dayne had released fourteen from their pain, each one like a knife through his heart. Eight of them had been children younger than Alina had been when he'd left.

The thought of Alina and Baren pricked up the hair on his arms, his chest tightening. He was so close. Once Sylvan Anura was dead, he could go back. He could protect his family, like he had failed to do before.

Exhaling through his nostrils, he turned back to face the ocean ahead only to find that they were approaching the pier, where a figure now stood, a man with short black hair flecked with white and grey, a beard covering most of his face. He wore a plain tunic with dark trousers, the hilts of two swords rising over his shoulders. Dayne recognised him immediately: Aeson Virandr.

As the ship pulled in against the pier and the oarsmen shipped their oars, replacing them with lengths of rope, Dayne's heart picked up its pace, growing louder with each beat until the rush of blood pushed out all other sounds. For a moment, Aeson's eyes locked with his, and Dayne knew that the man recognised him too.

"Aeson Virandr." Therin strode past Dayne, leaping from the deck of the ship onto the creaking wood of the pier.

Aeson stepped towards Therin, and they wrapped their arms around each other. "Therin Eiltris, with each day you look younger."

"It doesn't feel that way, old friend. Thank you for this."

"It's the least I could do. Especially considering the company you have brought." Aeson's eyes narrowed as Belina stepped past Dayne and lifted herself onto the pier. "Weapons stay on the boat."

"Aeson." Belina's voice took on the tone of a child pleading with their parent. "Be reasonable."

"On the boat."

Belina rested her hands on her hips, meeting Aeson's narrowed stare, before finally tilting her head back and sighing. One after another, she removed her sword belt, a knife from her right boot, another from the inside of her shirt, two strapped across her back, and finally one more from her left sleeve, tossing each one back into the boat as she did. "Happy?"

Aeson raised an eyebrow, unimpressed.

"Ugh, fine." Belina reached back and pulled a deceptively long steel needle from her hair, letting her locks fall down over her shoulders. Shrugging, she tossed it onto the pile of weapons in the ship. "You have trust issues, you know that?"

"You've tried to kill me six times, Belina."

"Seven," Belina corrected. "You're forgetting the bazaar in Vaerleon."

"You tried to kill me in the bazaar in Vaerleon?"

"… no?" Belina pursed her lips, staring towards the sky. "Either way, that was the old me. I don't work for the Hand anymore."

"I know. You have been busy, Belina. You both have." Aeson's gaze shifted to Dayne, who still stood on the deck of the ship, his mouth dry, his feet planted. "You have wreaked havoc on the Hand these last five years. My contacts in Berona say the Hand there calls you the Shadow's Blades. While those in Arkalen know you as the Ghosts of Ilragorn. You've built up quite the reputation. That doesn't mean I trust you."

"Fair," Belina said with a shrug. "I don't trust me either. I'm too unpredictable."

A knot formed in Dayne's throat as Aeson turned towards him. "Dayne Ateres. For a long time, I thought you were dead. It wasn't until I heard of Harsted Arnim's death that I began to suspect otherwise."

Drawing in a deep breath, Dayne stepped from the ship, balancing himself as he adjusted to the steadiness of the pier. He held Aeson's gaze for what felt like minutes but in reality was only seconds. "I blamed you," he said, a weight lifting from his shoulders. "For a long time, I blamed you for my parents' deaths – for all those who died at Stormwatch. You pushed my mother and father to rebel. You promised them the world. You promised us *all*, and then you weren't there when they needed you."

"What changed?" Aeson asked, his voice steady, his stare unyielding.

"Time passed." Dayne dropped his head, tracing his gaze along the cracks in the wood of the pier, before lifting it once more. "I saw the things the empire does in the South. I saw what they did to that child"—Dayne turned for a moment, looking towards the elven child who still sat with his knees tucked to his chest, his head twitching slightly—"and I asked myself, if you came to me now, the way you came to my parents, and you asked me to do it all again, what would I say?"

A silence hung in the air as Dayne's words lingered.

"What would you say, Dayne?"

"I would say that it is better to die for the ones you love and for what you believe than it is to live knowing that you could have done something but didn't. I would say that you have my sword. I would say that you have my blood. And if you can bring the empire to its knees, then I will gladly give you my life as well." Dayne could feel the tears streaming from his eyes, but he let them roll, feeling them pool at his chin before dripping to the pier below.

"It is never weak to grieve for the ones you love." Dayne's father had said that the day he had found Dayne weeping over the body of his grandmother. Dayne had tried to wipe away his tears, but his father had stayed his hand. *"To hide your tears is to do them a disservice. They have earned your love. Let them have it."*

Reaching out, Aeson grasped Dayne's forearm, meeting his tear-filled eyes. "You remind me so much of your father." The words were a hammer blow in Dayne's heart. "They were my friends, Dayne. And when you live as long as I have, you become very particular about those to whom you grant that title. I am sorry I was not there that night. I truly am. I have done everything in my power to put that right. I promise you."

Dayne nodded, swallowing hard, his throat constricting.

Aeson let go of Dayne's forearm, a weak smile on his face. "Come, the cabin is only a short walk."

"I will stay with the ship," Therin said, a sorrowful look in his eyes as he glanced towards the two elves, the elder cradling the child like a mother. "I will not leave them until I see them safe to Aravell." As though reading something in Aeson's expression, Therin added, "I will fill you in when all is done here."

Aeson nodded in acknowledgement before setting off down the pier.

As Dayne made to follow, Therin grasped his shoulder. He handed Dayne a small round-backed knife – the same one Dayne had seen him flipping across his fingers – and pressed Dayne's hand around the hilt. "I hope you find what you're looking for here, Dayne."

Dayne exhaled through his nostrils, nodding. "Me too, Therin."

With that, Therin climbed back aboard the ship, resting his back against the mast and sliding down to the deck, watching over the two elves who sat opposite him.

"Come on," Belina said, nudging her shoulder against Dayne's. "Let's go find out where this bitch is and how to kill her."

"You've a way with words, Belina. Have I ever told you that?"

"Not explicitly, but I read between the lines."

Despite her madness and penchant for inflicting physical pain, Belina always could make Dayne laugh.

The pier opened out onto a short beach of soft, greyish-white sand that quickly turned to stones before eventually becoming grass as they followed Aeson uphill. There was no path towards the house that sat at the top of the hill, not even so much as a track worn in the grass by footfall. This was not a place that saw many visitors, if any at all.

The house, comprised of stout pine logs and a thatched roof, rose no higher than a single storey.

Three steps led to a decked porch with a wooden rail, upon which was a young boy who stood with his arms crossed over the rail.

His hair was a dirty blonde, and he could not have seen any more than fourteen summers, and yet two swords were strapped across his back, and he wore a dark leather jerkin over a linen shirt, two knives strapped to a belt at his hip. He lifted his head as they approached, smiling.

Aeson led Dayne and Belina up the three steps to the deck, turning towards the young boy. "Belina, Dayne, this is my youngest, Erik. I'm not sure where my eldest, Dahlen, is." Aeson raised an eyebrow to his son.

"He's gone to get some more wood," Erik said, rolling his eyes. "He wasn't happy with his carving." The young boy gestured towards a half-carved block of wood that sat in a pile of shavings by the door. Dayne couldn't help but admire the craftsmanship of the carving. While it was only half finished, it was clear to be a dragon, each scale crafted with meticulous care, the frills along the back of its neck, delicate and thin.

"It's a pleasure to meet you both," Erik said, turning his attention towards Dayne and Belina, inclining his head.

"The pleasure is ours," Dayne said, tilting his head in response.

The young man's eyes narrowed as he looked closer at Belina. In a flash, he pulled a knife from his belt, pointing it towards Belina. "You're the one who attacked us in the forest outside Aeling, and you stalked us again in the bazaar in Vaerleon."

Without so much as flinching, Belina laughed, turning to Aeson. "I told you I was at the bazaar! Your child has good eyes."

"Lower the knife, son."

"But she tried to kill you," Erik argued, taking a step closer to Belina, the air changing slightly.

"I said lower the knife." Aeson rested his palm against the back of the blade, pushing it down. "You remember the story I told you of the Ghosts of Ilragorn, two summers past? Belina and Dayne are those ghosts. She walks a different path now."

"You tell your children stories about me? That's adorable."

"Your kills that night were quick and efficient. You used fear as a tool. It was a good lesson."

"Well... that's not so adorable."

Still eyeing Belina askance, Erik lowered his hand, slipping the knife into a sheath at his hip. "She's asked for you," he said, a frown on his face as he turned to his father.

"Who?" Belina tilted her head sideways.

Aeson rested his hand on his son's shoulder. "Stay out here, all right? Tell Dahlen to do the same if he comes back before I'm out."

The young man nodded, throwing one last glance towards Belina and Dayne before resting his arms back across the rail.

"Who was asking for you, Aeson?" Belina repeated.

Aeson sighed, his gaze lingering on Dayne. "Come, it's easier to show you."

The heat hit Dayne like a wall as he stepped into the house after Aeson. The air was thick and heavy, weighed down by the smell of charred wood, cooked meat, and sweat. Across from the doorway, two leather chairs sat before a roaring fireplace. The chair on the right was empty, but the chair on the left was occupied by a woman with long, dark hair staring into the flames, her hands laid against the armrests, trembling.

Another woman with brittle grey hair, time-furrowed skin, and liver-spotted hands stood between the fire and the woman in the chair. She held a thick woollen blanket in her hands, which she lay over the woman in the chair as gently as she would have with a newborn babe. Reaching down, the elderly woman grasped the other woman's hand, her fragile fingers squeezing. *A mother.*

At the sound of the door closing behind Belina, the elderly woman looked up, casting her gaze over the house's new occupants, gracing them with a smile that was both warm and deeply sorrowful. Dayne thought he had seen a tear rolling down the woman's cheek, glinting in the firelight as she inclined her head towards Aeson, let go of the other woman's hand, and hobbled from the room.

His eyes following the elderly woman as she left, Aeson made his way to the window set into the wall on the left side of the room, folding his arms across his chest as he looked out over the ocean. "After what happened to Stormwatch and your parents, I spent the following years tracking down the Dragonguard involved. In the last century, they have grown lax, thinking themselves gods among mortals. This made them vulnerable. With Therin's aid, and the aid of many others who no longer draw breath, I slew Marek Tarn at Dead Rock's Hold. I put one blade through her heart and another through her gut. The dragon to which she was bound, Nyrnin, lost his sight and his fire when she was taken from him. I freed him of his pain, and the mountains are where their bodies rest."

A knot twisted in Dayne's chest as Aeson spoke, chills running through him.

"Johan Finik sent twelve of my companions from this world when we found him at the foothills of Mar Dorul. But after I drove a spear of stone through his soulkin's skull, he begged me to end his life. I obliged."

Dayne's mouth was as dry as sand, his chest trembling. "What of Sylvan Anura?"

For a long moment, Aeson said nothing. He continued to stare out the window, allowing the silence to consume the room. "I found Sylvan one year ago, in Catagan. She was visiting her daughter."

Dayne's heart skipped a beat. He had found her. "That's where she is then, in Catagan?"

Aeson shook his head. "She is not."

"Why do you play games?" Dayne could do nothing to stop the anger from rising, the muscles in his neck tensing. He clenched his fingers into a fist, trying to stop his hand from shaking. "Tell me where she is!"

Aeson let out a sigh, turning away from the window. "I followed her for months. Each week she would visit Catagan, and each week she would leave her soulkin, Aramel, on a cliff's edge some twenty miles south. I waited, and I watched. Until four months ago, when I crept to the cliff's edge where the dragon slept."

The rage that had been bubbling in Dayne's blood subsided at the sight of the abject grief in Aeson's eyes.

"I do not know what knowledge you have of the bond between a dragon and a Draleid. It is not simply a kinship. It is an intertwining of souls – a blending of hearts and minds so complete that the loss of one can break the other beyond reckoning." Aeson drew in a deep breath, trying to settle himself. "It took almost seven hours for Sylvan to reach the cliff's edge. She dragged herself over the jagged rock, crawled to her soulkin's lifeless body, and collapsed beside him, quivering. To call the sound that left her mouth a scream would be to call thunder a whisper."

Suddenly, Dayne's chest emptied to a hollow, and his heart sank into the pit of his stomach. A shiver ran the length and breadth of his body, starting in his chest and sweeping outward. He drew a trembling breath, turning away from Aeson, his gaze resting on the woman in the chair. "It can't be…" he whispered, his lips dry as bone.

Belina rested her hand on his shoulder as he took a step towards the fireplace, but he ignored her. He could feel his heart thumping, hammering with every step.

"When Aramel was taken from her," Aeson continued, "she was stripped of the ability to hear, the warmth was dragged from her body, and an unyielding tremble set into her limbs."

Dayne's blood ran cold in his veins as he drew closer to the woman in the chair, the warmth from the fire touching his skin.

"When she finally lifted her head and saw me standing there, Aramel's blood dripping from my blades, she drew so heavily from the Spark that the mountain itself shook, and the rock cracked. She drew on far more than any one person could have handled. I watched as her eyes ignited in a blaze of light and the Spark was burned from her body, taking her sight with it."

Rounding the chair, standing between the woman and the fireplace, Dayne found himself staring down at a face that had been etched in his mind for seven years: Sylvan Anura. Her skin was the same deep brown, her hair black as night, but where dark eyes had once been, now sat two knotted sockets of burned flesh.

"Part of me wanted to end her life right then and there," Aeson continued. "To show her the mercy I showed Johan. But I carried her from that cliff, brought her from Catagan to Kingspass, and chartered a ship to this island."

Dayne almost hadn't noticed his hand drifting to the knife Therin had given him, which was hanging from his belt, his fingers brushing the steel. He let his hand hover there as he stared at Sylvan. The entire time, she hadn't moved. Both her hands trembled against the leather arm rests, her eyeless gaze staring past Dayne. He almost stumbled backwards when she spoke.

"If you're going to kill me, do it. I cannot hear, and I cannot see. But I can feel your footsteps through the floor, and I can feel your breath on my skin."

Dayne pulled the knife from his belt, his hand trembling. He remembered that night as clear as anything. He remembered the feel of the rope against his skin, the touch of the breeze on his face. He remembered the fire and the screams. He remembered Sylvan's blade as it punched through his father's chest, and he remembered the look on his mother's face as her head was taken from her shoulders.

"You took everything from me…" He stepped closer to Sylvan, his fingers tightening on the hilt of the knife, knuckles turning white. All it would take was one motion. One slice of the blade and her blood would stain the leather of the chair. He angled the blade, pressing it against her neck, drawing forth a thin stream of blood. Dayne tightened his grip on the knife as Sylvan turned her head towards him, her eyeless gaze fixing on him for a moment before she tilted her head upwards, exposing her neck.

"You are not Aeson Virandr." Each word lingered on the woman's tongue, slow and purposeful. She pressed her neck harder against the blade of the knife. "Do what you came here to do."

Dayne clenched his jaw, attempting to still the trembling breaths that left his lungs. Seven years he had hunted this woman. Seven years he had wanted to drain the blood from her body. And now here she was, before him, blind, deaf, cut off from the Spark, and her dragon gone. It should have been simple, and yet…

He watched as the light from the fire cast shadows over her face. Her cheeks quivered as though attempting to summon tears from eyes that no longer were. Sylvan Anura. That name had haunted him for so long. The mighty Dragonguard. The woman who took his parents and exiled him from his home. She, who rode astride a beast from legend. But this was not Sylvan Anura. Not anymore. This woman was nothing more than a ghost in a shell.

Slowly, he pulled the blade from her neck, his hand shaking.

"No," the woman growled through gritted teeth before her voice rose to a shout. "No!"

Dayne had expected her to lunge at him, to push him, to strike him, but instead, she leaned back into the chair, pulled her knees to her chest and sobbed. No tears fell down her cheeks, but her shoulders convulsed and her body trembled, harsh whimpers escaping her throat.

Dayne stood for a few moments, watching the architect of his nightmares whimper and sob. Part of him felt pity, but another part enjoyed every second of her misery. He pulled his eyes from the weeping wretch. Belina stood a few feet away, by the door, her eyes wide and her mouth open. But Aeson's face held no such shock; his was that of a man who had seen precisely what he had expected to see.

As Dayne saw the sorrow that pooled in Aeson's eyes, he finally understood. "You brought her here so she would be forced to live."

Aeson turned away, fixing his gaze on something in the corner of the room, giving the slightest nod of his head. "To lose your soulkin… to feel that emptiness, that hollow in the centre of your being. I wanted her to feel that. I wanted her to *always* feel that."

Leaving the woman sobbing in the chair, Dayne stepped closer to Aeson. "Therin said you used to be one of them… a Draleid."

Aeson bit the corner of his lip. "Lyara was taken from me three hundred and ninety-one winters ago. We were hunted right here to this very spot…" Aeson trailed off as though lost in a living memory. "There were five of them and two of us. The bones of six dragons and five Draleid lay on this island." Tears rolled down Aeson's cheeks as he spoke, his eyes reddening. "In the end, it was only Lyara and I, and Sylvan and Aramel."

"You fought Sylvan? Here?"

Aeson nodded absently. "I felt Lyara die. I…" He lifted his gaze, his bloodshot eyes staring into Dayne's. "I could *feel* her fear. She was so scared… and then she was gone, and I was alone. Her last gift to me was tearing so deeply into Aramel's chest that he and Sylvan had no choice but to flee. We crashed down right here, on this very spot. It was a valley then, but I built the hill around her. I can still feel her when I'm here… echoes, shadows. I don't know what they are, but I don't feel so broken when I'm here."

Dayne's heart ached. "Why… why did you bring *her* here? You should have thrown her in a cage and locked her in a pit."

"So she can live broken in the place where she broke me. So she can live *every* second of her long life and feel every single drop of pain."

"Who is the woman?" Dayne asked, remembering the elderly woman who had been tending to Sylvan when they had entered. Surely, she could not be Sylvan's mother.

"That is Anees. Sylvan's daughter. She cares for her, feeds her, bathes her – keeps her alive. That was part of our deal."

"Daughter… but she's…"

If it was possible, Aeson's eyes seemed to take on an even deeper sadness, a weak smile touching his lips. "Such is the curse of a long life. While the years turn to decades and decades turn to centuries, you watch those you love wither and die, slowly worn away by the passing of time.

No parent should live to see their child grow old, but this is the way."

Dayne's chest tightened as he thought of Aeson's two children, one of whom stood on the deck outside the house. That was Dayne's future too. Even if Mera were to welcome him back with open arms after all this time, he would never grow old with her. He would never share that with her. The Spark would not allow it. "What will happen when Anees dies? Who will keep Sylvan alive then?"

"I will arrange something. She will not escape this fate."

Dayne looked back towards the sobbing mess of a woman, the warm fire light casting shifting shadows across her eyeless face, her shoulders convulsing, her whimpers fading to a low sniffle. He nodded, then headed for the door.

"Where are you going?" Aeson called after him, but Dayne didn't stop. He walked straight past Belina and stepped through the doorway.

The cold air sent chills through Dayne's body as he stepped from the house. He didn't so much as glance towards Aeson's son, Erik, but he could feel the boy's eyes on him. He stumbled as he stepped off the deck, his legs shaking, his lungs trembling. A storm swept through him as he dropped to his knees. Leaning forwards, he wrapped his fingers around tufts of grass and ripped them from the earth, screaming until his voice cracked and tears streamed from his eyes. Seven years he had hunted Sylvan. All that time, her blood was all he wanted. Vengeance. Vengeance for his mother. Vengeance for his father. Vengeance for everything she had taken from him. But when he had held that blade to her neck and saw the whimpering mess she had become, it had all just felt… empty.

"Dayne…" Belina's voice trailed off. He could hear her feet against the steps of the deck, her arms wrapping around him from behind. For some reason, that meant more to him than anything else she could have said or done.

Kneeling there with Belina's arms around him, he wept, for it was all he could bring himself to do. After a few moments, he steadied himself, drawing in a deep breath and stilling the tears. "I'm going home." The words lingered on his tongue, feeling strange yet welcome. He pulled Belina's arms from around him and turned to her. "Sylvan is as good as dead. I will drive a knife through Loren Koraklon's heart, and I will finish what my parents started."

"I'm coming with you." Belina nodded as she spoke, staring into Dayne's eyes.

"You don't have to—"

"Shut up," Belina interrupted. "Every time you open your mouth, you say something stupid. I'm coming with you, Dayne. I've killed enough people for money and power. It's time I do it for a good reason. Besides, I need to meet this 'Mera'." A smile crept across Belina's face as those last words left her mouth.

Dayne smiled back, wiping away the last of the tears from his cheek he grasped Belina's forearm. "By blade and by blood."

"Does everyone in Valtara say that as much as you? Oh, fine, by blade and by blood." Belina reciprocated the gesture, wrapping her fingers around Dayne's fore-arm, both of them rising to their feet.

"I would advise against that."

Dayne looked up to find Aeson descending the deck steps towards them. He could feel his blood start to heat, his jaw clenching. "And why is that?" Dayne pushed past Belina, standing in front of Aeson, their eyes level. "Why would I leave my brother and sister to stand alone when I can be by their side? Why would I allow Loren Koraklon to draw any more breaths than I have to? And why would I leave my people under the boot of the empire?"

"Because if you return, it will all be for nothing. Any rebellion now will be crushed, shattered by imperial steel and broken beneath the Dragonguard."

"You don't stop fighting just because someone says you can't win. You fight harder."

"I'm not asking you not to fight. I'm just asking you to wait. Give me time to give you a real chance."

"And how will you do that, Aeson? Your plans failed my parents. I don't blame you, but that doesn't mean I will follow you blindly."

Aeson took a step towards Dayne. "I failed your par-ents, Dayne, and I'm sorry. I cannot change what has already been done, but if you go back now, if you start this war before you are ready, then you will join them in Achyron's halls, as will your brother and your sister. And Valtara will never be free. That is not what your parents fought for."

You, your brothers, and your sister are the best things I ever did with my life. Look after each other, Dayne. He could hear his mother's words in his mind as though they were both still standing on the deck of that ship.

"Give me the time I need. Let me teach you how to truly use your power. Let me gather those who can light the spark of rebellion across the continent. Do this, and Valtara will be free. I promise you."

For a long moment, Dayne stared into Aeson's eyes. All he wanted was to return home, to hold Baren and Alina in his arms and to break the chains around his people's necks. But there was truth in Aeson's words. Sylvan might not be able to stop him, but if he killed Loren Koraklon and led his people to rebellion, the Dragonguard would simply do as they had done before. And Dayne knew in his heart of hearts that were he to return home, there wasn't a chance he could allow Loren to continue drawing breath. To return home would be to start a war. One they were likely to lose. "What is different about your plan? How will it succeed where mine would fail?"

Aeson took another step closer, clasping his hands onto Dayne's shoulders. "We will light a fire in the hearts of all those who suffer. Not just Valtara. Drifaien, Illyanara, Arkalen, Varsund, Carvahon. We will not simply give the empire one fire to snuff out, we will ignite a rebellion that spans the continent. We will spread them so thin they tear themselves apart."

"That's all well and good, Aeson, but how?"

"We give them a symbol, something to rally behind. Hope," Aeson said, a smile spreading across his face. "Give people hope, and they *will* fight."

"Pretty words, but you still haven't answered – *how?*"

"Have you heard of the dragons of Valacia?"

IX

THE LETTER

FIVE YEARS LATER

Marin Mountains
Year 3080 after doom

Dayne felt as though he could hear every sound in the world as he sat on the edge of the cliff. The threads of Air and Spirit that weaved around him amplified every vibration that rippled through the air. He could hear each separate beat of the humming-bird's wings as it prowled a nearby tree for insects. The slow breaths of the fox and its cubs as they slept in their den nearby. The crunch of dirt beneath the feet of the goat who trotted along the path forty feet below. The sound of the animal's beating heart, a war drum. Its breathing like the rush of forge bellows. With every step, it drew nearer, the sounds of its existence growing louder and louder, until its footsteps were like claps of thunder in his mind.

Drawing in a deep breath, he opened his eyes and released the Spark, wincing as his eyes adjusted to the harsh light from the morning sun above.

Sighing, he looked at the letter that sat on his lap, sealed with blue wax stamped with the symbol of two crossed blades. He ran his fingers across the envelope's surface, the paper coarse against his fingertips. He was sure Belina would receive a similar letter soon, if she had not already. It had been weeks since Dayne had seen her. She had gone to resolve a 'family matter' in Argona and had asked him to stay put. He didn't like it, but he respected it. Besides, a few weeks without her incessant talking wasn't the worst thing he could think of.

Steadying himself for just a moment, Dayne broke the seal with his fingers and slipped the letter from the envelope. The moisture in his mouth evaporated, his throat growing tighter. He bit into his lip so hard the taste of blood coated his tongue. He peeled the letter open.

Dayne,

I asked you to give me time, and you did. For that, I thank you. I know the wait has not been easy.

I promised you Valtara would be free. I promised you I would light the spark of rebellion across the entire continent. I promised you hope.

It is time, Dayne. Not only have we succeeded in bringing the egg back from Valacia, but a new Draleid has already been bound. He is young, brash, and touched by pain. But he is also determined, loyal, and has a lot of potential. I see much of you in him. He is to be our symbol. Our hope. I have sent letters across the continent to those who would light the spark. To succeed, we will need Valtara.

There is a new dawn on the horizon, Dayne. We will break the empire's hold on the continent, and we will grind them to dust.

It's time for you to go home.

A

Acknowledgments

It's been just over a year since I started on this writing journey. Sharing the depths of my imagination with the world. *The Exile* is the fourth book to be born in that time, and I'm damn proud of it, and the series as a whole so far.

It's been a whirlwind of a year. I've gotten engaged, moved continent, bought a house, and started a new career – all in the middle of a global pandemic. There have been some low lows, and some high highs. It's been equal parts tough and rewarding.

With that, there are a few people who have helped me through to this point. People who have carried, pushed, pulled, and dragged me (out of bed).

Robin. You were the bestest girl that ever was. You were beautiful, intelligent, playful, and you had more party tricks than a career clown. You were also grumpy, sassy, and forever moody. You were Valerys. You were Faenir. You were perfect. Forever in my heart.

Amy. You brought me to Middle Earth and bought a hobbit hole with me. You inspire me. You push me to be better. You make great muffins. You are my Ayar Elwyn.

Séamus. This has been a strange time where we have spent most of the year separated by thousands of miles. But even then, our calls and chats have rarely been separated by anything more than days. Still my ride or die biatch.

My parents. I've probably thanked you enough at this stage, though I doubt you would agree. I might be far away right now, but you will always be my home.

My brother, Aron. Shithead. Your art continues to grow to new heights. But so do you as a person. You're not half bad.

Sarah, my editor – writer mom. It's been a tough year, but we're still here. Shouting, kicking, and screaming. Because that's what we do. We take everything that seeks to destroy us, grab it by the throat, look it in the eyes, and say, "Fuck you. I'm Sarah Chorn and you can't touch me." Well, I don't say 'I'm Sarah Chorn', you do. But you get the idea.

My Beta readers: Mark, Roy, Kristin, Adam, Ross, Gina, Viv, Brian, Kenny, Carol, Sannie, Josie, and Blaise. You were absolutely instrumental in helping to craft this book into what it is. I could say thank you every day for the rest of my life and wouldn't be enough.

My Advance Readers: Blaise, Johan, Josie, Brian, Kristin, Will, Melissa, Tianna, Craig, Brenda, Anthony, Rachael, Chase, Peter, Dom, Mike, Evan, Winter, Jamie, Pat, Graham, Emma, Becky, Alicia, Dave, David, Eddie, John, Donna, Robert, Terry, Dylan, Marie, Steve, Simon, Yann, Jason, Rashmi, Beki. Thank you for your unabating support, for travelling this path with me, and for always waving my flag. There are of course many more of you, all of whom hold a place in my heart. May your fires never be extinguished and your blades never dull.

To all of you. Yes, each and every one of you who have read my books. Thank you. You've allowed me to live my dream. I get to tell stories for a living. My younger self would be so damn happy right now. *The Exile* is one more step on this path, but it's far from the last.

Glossary

Arkin Ateres (ARE-KIN AH-Teer-eece): Head of House Ateres. Husband of Ilya Ateres, father of Alina, Dayne, Baren, and Owain.

Ilya Ateres (IL-YAH AH-Teer-eece): Commander of the Wyvern Rider's of Valtara. Wife of Arkin Ateres, mother of Alina, Dayne, Baren, and Owain.

Dayne Ateres (DAIN AH-Teer-eece): Son of Arkin and Ilya Ateres, brother of Alina, Baren, and Owain. Heir to House Ateres.

Alina Ateres (AH-leen-AH AH-teer-eece): Daughter of Arkin and Ilya Ateres, sister of Dayne, Baren, and Owain.

Baren Ateres (BAH-REN Ah-teer-eece): Son of Arkin and Ilya Ateres, brother of Alina, Dayne, and Owain.

Owain Ateres (OH-AY-in Ah-teer-eece): Son of Arkin and Ilya Ateres, brother of Alina, Dayne, and Baren. Given over to the empire as a child.

Mera Vardas (MEH-RAH VAR-DAS): Aligned with House Ateres. Close friend of Alina, past lover of Dayne.

Aeyrin Vardas (AYE-RIN VAR-DAS): Aligned with House Ateres. Head tailor of House Ateres. Mother of Mera, widow of Lukeer Vardas.

Marlin Arkon (Mar-lin ARE-kon): Steward of House Ateres.

Savrin Vander (sav-RIN van-DER): Champion of House Ateres.

Iloen Akaida (IH-low-EN AH-kay-DAH): Porter in the Redstone kitchens. Son of Sora and Aren Akaida.

Loren Koraklon (Loh-REN KUH-RAK-lon): Head of House Koraklon.

Harsted Arnim (HAR-STEHD ARE-NIM): Commander of the Lorian Fifth Army.

Belina Louna (BELL-eena Loo-NAH): A bard that played in the feast tent after The Proving.

Fane Mortem (FAIN MORE-tem): Emperor of Loria.

Therin Eiltris (Theh-RIN EHL-treece): Former elven ambassador to The Order, powerful mage.

Aeson Virandr (Ay-son VIR-an-DUR): Former Draleid whose dragon was slain, and is now Rakina. Father of Dahlen and Erik.

Dahlen Virandr (DAH-lin VIR-an-DUR): Son of Aeson, brother of Erik.

Erik Virandr (AIR-ICK VIR-an-DUR): Son of Aeson, brother of Dahlen.

Eltoar Daethana (EL-TWAR Die-THA-NAH): Commander of the Dragonguard. Bonded to Helios. Wing commander of Lyina and Pellenor.

Lyina (Lie-eee-NAH): Member of the Dragonguard. Bonded to Karakes. Eltoar's left wing.

Pellenor (Pel-EH-NOR): Member of the Dragonguard. Bonded to Meranth. Eltoar's right wing.

Sylvan Anura: Member of the Dragonguard. Bonded to Aramel. Wing Commander of Marek Tarn and Johan Finik.

Marek Tarn: Bonded to Nyrnin. Sylvan's right wing.

Johan Finik: Bonded to unnamed dragon. Sylvan's left wing.

The Gods

Achyron (Ack-er-on): The warrior God, or simply The Warrior. The protector against the shadow.

Elyara (El-eee-ARE-AH): The Maiden. The wisest of all the gods, creator of consciousness and free thought.

Varyn (Var-in): The Father. The protector of all things and the provider of the sun.

Heraya (HER-eye-AH): The Mother. The giver of life and receiver of the dead.

Hafaesir (Hah-FYE-SEER): The Smith. The Patron god of the dwarves. Builder of the world.

Neron (NEH-ron): The Sailor. Creator of the seas and provider of safe travel.

Efialtír (Ef-EE-ahl-TIER): The Traitor God. Efialtír betrayed the other six gods at the dawn of creation. He turned his back on their ways, claiming his power through offerings of blood.

The Old Tongue

Draleid (Drah-laid): Dragonbound. Ancient warriors whose souls were bonded to the dragons that hatched for them.

Rakina (Rah-KEEN-ah): One who is broken, or in the elven dialect – 'one who survived'. When a dragon or their Draleid dies, the other earns the title of 'Rakina'.

Du gryr haydria til myia elwyn (DOO Greer HAY-dree-AH till MAYA EHL-win): You bring honour to my heart.

N'aldryr (Nahl-DREAR): By fire.

Valerys (Vah-lair-is): Ice.

Det være myia haydria (Deh-t VAY-air MAYA HAY-dree-AH): *It would be my honour.*

Du haryn myia vrai (Doo Hah-RIN MAYA VRAY): *You have my thanks.*

Myia elwyn er unira diar *(MAYA EHL-win AIR OO-neer-AH Dee-ARE):* My heart is always yours.

Din vrai é atuya sin'vala (DIN VRAY Eh AH-too-YAH Sin-VAH-LAH): *Your thanks are welcome here.*

Draleid n'aldryr, Rakina nai dauva (Drah-laid Nahl-DREAR, Rah-KEEN-ah Nay D-ow-VAH): *Dragon-bound by fire, broken by death.*

Det er aldin na vëna du (Deh-t AIR Ahl-DIN Nah VAY-na DOO): *It is good to see you.*

Myia nithír til diar (MAYA NIH-theer TILL Dee-ARE): *My soul to yours.*

I denír viël ar altinua (Eee Deh-Neer Vee-EL ARE Al-tin-OO-AH): *In this life and always.*

Vaen (VAY-en): *Truth.*

Drunir (DREW-Neer): *Companion.*

Aldryr (ALL-DREAR): Fire.

Níthral (Nee-TH-ral): Soulblade.

Svidar'Cia (Svih-DAR-see-AH): *Burnt Lands.*

Svidarya (Svih-DAR-eee-AH): *Burning Winds.*

Valacia (VAH-lay-see-AH): *Icelands.*

Nithír (NIH-Theer): *Soul.*

Din haydria er fyrir (DIN HAY-dree-AH AIR Fih-reer): *Your honour is forfeit.*

Bralgír (Brahl-GEER): *Storyteller.*

Ayar Elwyn (Ay-ARE EHL-win): One Heart.

Galdrín (GAHL-DREEN): *Mage.*

Idyn väe (IH-din VAY): *Rest well.*

Du vyin alura anis (DOO vie-IN ah-LOOR-ah ah-NEECE): *You can rest now.*

Races

Humans: Humans first arrived on the continent of Epheria in the year 306 After Doom, fleeing from an unknown cataclysm in their homeland of Terroncia.

Elves: Along with the Jotnar and the dwarves, the elves were one of the first races to inhabit Epheria. After the fall of the Order the elves fought valiantly against the newly formed Lorian Empire, but were eventually defeated and subsequently split into two major factions. One faction blamed the humans for the decimation of Epheria, and retreated into the enormous woodland known as Lynalion, withdrawing themselves from the rest of the continent. The other faction withdrew to the Darkwood, where they built the city of Aravell and continued on the fight in secret by turning the Darkwood into an impassable barrier between the North and South.

Dwarves: Before the fall of The Order, the dwarves occupied territories both above land and below. But after The Fall, the dwarves retreated back to their mountain kingdoms for safety.

Uraks (UH–raks): Creatures whose way of life revolves around bloodshed. Little is known of them outside of battle, other than they serve the traitor God – Efialtír.

Jotnar (Jot–Nar): The Jotnar, known to humans as 'giants', are a race of people who have inhabited Epheria since the dawn of time. They are intrinsically magic, have bluish-white skin, and stand over eight feet tall.

Angan (Ann–GAN): The Angan are a race of humanoid shapeshifters. It is not truly known when they arrived in Epheria, though it is thought that they are as old as the land itself. They are divided into five major factions, each devoted to one of the five Angan Gods: Dvalin, Bjorna, Vethnir, Fenryr, and Kaygan.